"What do you see in the mirror, Phoebe?"

Phoebe saw an incredibly hot man more than capable of giving her a sexual adventure.

That's probably not what Heath means.

With their bodies so close, could he feel the quiver that went through her? She was turned on, and the longer they stood together, the more the ache of arousal intensified.

"You have great hair and a great neck, too." Heath trailed his knuckles across the curve of her neck. "Gives a man ideas. About doing this."

Transfixed, she watched him lower his dark head toward her, anticipation coiling tighter until his teeth grazed an excruciatingly sensitive spot behind her jaw. The woman in the mirror was flushed, her lips parted, her hardened nipples visible through the silk of the tank top.

Her total focus was on the dual sensations of his mouth hot on her skin and the rock-hard erection pressed against her.

Phoebe might not be an experienced seductress or the type of woman who had leather in her lingerie drawer, but she'd sure as hell aroused Heath...

Dear Reader,

I live in the South, where the summers are incredibly steamy. Just when you think it can't get any hotter, the temperature rises a little more... which I used as my inspiration for the relationship between pastry chef Phoebe Mars and sexy restaurant owner Heath Jensen.

Recently jilted by a critically acclaimed chef, Phoebe dreads running into him at a party. When Heath Jensen kisses her to help make her ex jealous, she's stunned—especially by how hot the kiss is. Knowing that she's playing with fire but unable to resist, she agrees with Heath's suggestion that they pretend to be dating. Not only will it help salvage her pride and show her ex what he's missing, she's learning a lot about the art of seduction from Heath.

But when the three of them end up in Miami to scout a new restaurant location, Phoebe and Heath's pretend affair becomes very real...and *very* hot.

Friends-to-lovers books are among my favorite to write (probably because I married my best friend!) and I'd love to hear what you think of Phoebe and Heath's story. Drop me an email at booksbytanya@gmail.com or follow me on Twitter (@tanyamichaels) to chat about books, TV and my dog's ongoing plot to murder me by tripping me on the staircase.

Happy reading!

Tanya

Tanya Michaels

Turning Up the Heat

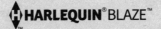

Recycling programs
for this product may
not exist in your area.

ISBN-13: 978-0-373-79901-5

Turning Up the Heat

Copyright © 2016 by Tanya Michna

This edition published by arrangement with Harlequin Books S.A.

For questions and comments about the quality of this book, please contact us at CustomerService@Harlequin.com.

Printed in U.S.A.

Tanya Michaels, a *New York Times* bestselling author and five-time RITA® Award nominee, has been writing love stories since middle-school algebra class (which probably explains her math grades). Her books, praised for their poignancy and humor, have received awards from readers and reviewers alike. Tanya is an active member of Romance Writers of America and a frequent public speaker. She lives outside Atlanta with her very supportive husband, two highly imaginative kids and a bichon frise who thinks she's the center of the universe.

Books by Tanya Michaels

Harlequin Blaze

Good with His Hands
If She Dares

Harlequin American Romance

Hill Country Heroes

Claimed by a Cowboy
Tamed by a Texan
Rescued by a Ranger

The Colorado Cades

Her Secret, His Baby
Second Chance Christmas
Her Cowboy Hero

Texas Rodeo Barons

The Texan's Christmas

Cupid's Bow, Texas

Falling for the Sheriff
Falling for the Rancher

To get the inside scoop on Harlequin Blaze and its talented writers, be sure to check out BlazeAuthors.com.

All backlist available in ebook format.

Visit the Author Profile page at Harlequin.com for more titles.

Thank you to Trish Milburn, who has been there for me in countless ways—including brainstorming naughty books over the phone at one in the morning.

1

"I DON'T KNOW which is the bigger betrayal—that you called my boss behind my back, or that you did it first thing in the morning." Phoebe Mars shoved her hair out of her face to make sure her roommate got the full effect of her glare.

Completely unapologetic, Gwen sat on the edge of the queen bed and handed her the cordless phone. "I'm allowed to call him. I knew him first, remember?"

True. After Gwen had introduced her to James Falk last year, he'd joked for months about stealing Phoebe away from her pastry-chef job to design signature desserts for All the Right Notes, a tapas bar that featured live music and wine tastings. He'd been stunned when she'd actually taken him up on it three weeks ago—although, not as stunned as she'd been by what had happened after she'd changed jobs.

She cleared her throat, trying to sound awake and articulate. "Hello?"

An exuberant person, James didn't waste time on small talk. "Why didn't you tell me it was one of your closest friend's birthdays?" he demanded. "I insist you take the night off and go to the party!"

Gwendolyn Yeager, you are a dead woman. Gwen knew perfectly well why Phoebe didn't want to attend that party. "But Saturday night is our busiest," she protested, "and—"

"Honey, I adore you—almost as much as the customers adore your desserts—but we survived for months without you. We'll survive this one night. After what you've been through, you deserve some fun."

He meant her broken heart. Perhaps Gwen had neglected to mention that Phoebe's ex would *also* be at the party. Seeing him would be the opposite of fun. It had been ten days, but the breakup still felt more like a bad dream than reality.

She wasn't ready to face him. "How about I come in for a couple of hours but don't work my full shift?" The offer was only partially motivated by cowardice. James was a dream to work for and she didn't want to let him down.

"Not a chance. Gwen requested prep time to help you get ready. You are going to walk into that party at your most fabulous and show that ex of yours what he's missing."

Ah. So James did know. *They ambushed me.*

"Gotta run," James said, "but Steve and I want to hear all the details tomorrow!" The line went dead.

Dropping the phone on the pale blue comforter, Phoebe turned to her roommate. "I hate you."

"I can live with that."

"And I'm getting a dead bolt for my bedroom door," she proclaimed.

"We'll pick one up while we're out. Now you go shower while I make coffee. We have a big day of shopping ahead of us."

"Ugh." Phoebe flopped backward, pulling her pillow over her face. She loved shopping for recipe ingredients and kitchen supplies, but she doubted Gwen was taking her to look at infrared candy thermometers.

Gwen poked her in the shoulder. "You remember how determined you were in high school that you were going to tutor me into passing the geometry final? *That's* how determined I am now. As far as I'm concerned, how a woman looks when she runs into her ex for the first time is tied in importance with how a bride looks on her wedding day."

Weddings—the end result of getting engaged. Behind the pillow, Phoebe's eyes watered. In hindsight, it was hilarious how wrong she'd been about her last date with Cam.

Painfully, agonizingly hilarious.

In addition to being lovers for two years, she and Chef Cameron Pala had been colleagues, working together at Piri, the newest Atlanta hotspot. Last month, Cam had begun hinting that if they were ever going to move in together or get married, maybe it would be healthier for their relationship if they didn't also work together. So she'd taken the job at All the Right Notes. After she'd been there a few days, Cam had taken her for a walk in Piedmont Park, where they'd met. When he'd reached for her hand, his expression unusually somber, she'd actually believed...

Gwen lifted the corner of the pillow. "In retrospect, it was insensitive of me to mention brides, but you don't *really* want to get married, Pheeb. You're only twenty-five. Settle down in your thirties. Our twenties are the perfect time for wild, sexy adventures!"

The corner of Phoebe's mouth twitched. Gwen had held a similar philosophy during their teenage years. "We have to live life to the fullest before we turn into boring adults, Pheeb," she'd said. Her friend had been an audacious blonde bombshell since high school; she'd also been a sanity-saving counterbalance to Phoebe's bitter mother.

Grateful for years of Gwen's friendship, Phoebe sat up, pledging her cooperation. "All right. Make me fabulous." If anyone could, it was Gwen Yeager, professional makeup artist. She worked on a television show that was shot outside Atlanta and occasionally freelanced for movies that filmed in the area.

"Yes!" With a triumphant smile, Gwen scrambled off the bed. "I can't wait to find you the perfect dress. As relieved as I was when you *finally* stopped wearing baggy cargo pants—"

"They were considered fashionable when we were in high school."

"—you still hide your bod in those long-sleeved, double-breasted jackets."

"All chefs wear them!"

"Not tonight." Gwen's blue eyes lit with glee. "Tonight, you are a Gwen Yeager creation. Cameron will fall to his knees and beg you to take him back."

"You really think so?" Traitorous hope warmed her heart.

"He's absolutely going to want you back—if not today, then soon. You're the best thing to ever happen to him." She frowned. "The real question is, can you forgive him for hurting you like that?"

"I don't know." But Phoebe desperately wanted the chance to find out.

"FINALLY, HEATH JENSEN ARRIVES! *Now* it's a party." Bobbi Barrett, the guest of honor and Heath's favorite food blogger, greeted him with a wide grin and stretched up on tiptoe to kiss his cheek.

"Happy birthday, beautiful." Heath scanned the room over her shoulder, impressed that Bobbi and her boyfriend had been able to cram so many people into their Buckhead condo. Guests filled the living room and kitchen and spilled out onto the balcony. A brunette he was pretty sure he'd slept with waved at him from her perch on the arm of a low-backed sofa. "Quite a crowd. Not worried the neighbors will complain?"

"Of course not. The neighbors were the first people we invited."

"Smart. Where can I put this?" He held up the small gold box containing her birthday present.

"Ooh, I'll take that!" She eyed the box speculatively, as if trying to guess its contents. "But you know the only gift you had to get me was a reservation. Booking a table at Piri is next to impossible. You and Cam must be thrilled."

Heath had always believed the upscale Portuguese-fusion restaurant he'd opened with Chef Cameron Pala would be successful—he never would have invested such a significant chunk of money otherwise—but buzz had spread even faster than he'd hoped. "You don't need a reservation. You're welcome anytime."

"In that case, you're officially my favorite person. Just don't tell everyone else." She lowered her voice to a confidential whisper. "Speaking of my other guests, I should warn you that the Kemp sisters have been doing shots. Brace yourself—they have a bet going on which one of them you'll take home tonight."

"How high are the stakes? I'd hate for anyone to lose on my account. Seems like the gentlemanly thing to do would be to invite them *both* back to my place."

Bobbi smacked his arm. "You are terrible."

"Maybe I'm just misunderstood." He gazed into her eyes, making a halfhearted attempt to keep a straight face. "How do you know my torrid love life isn't an attempt to comfort myself because I'm secretly pining for you and cursing that Matt met you first?"

"Did I hear my name?" Matt Grantham slid an arm around Bobbi's waist and nuzzled her neck.

"I was just telling Bobbi that you're the envy of all the single straight men in Atlanta," Heath said. "She's a hell of a woman."

Matt nodded. "Gorgeous, smart, funny and dy-namite in b—*oof.*" He grunted when Bobbi's elbow connected with his rib cage.

She shot him a stern look, but the twitch of her lips showed she was fighting a smile. "That's more than enough about me. Matt, why don't you get Heath a drink while I mingle?"

"What's your poison?" Matt asked, leading Heath to a bar in the corner of the living room.

Studying the selection of liquors, Heath chose a top-shelf bourbon. While Matt poured, they exchanged opinions on the baseball season. Heath was analyzing the Braves' pitching when he caught a flash of familiar red-gold waves in his peripheral vision. *Phoebe?* Last time he'd talked to her, she'd said she had to work and wouldn't be here tonight. Nonetheless, he tried to get a better look at the woman as she stepped outside through the open balcony doors. He'd never seen Phoebe wear anything as short as that glittery navy dress, yet recognition sparked through him.

His gaze dipped to her heart-shaped ass and supple legs. Definitely Phoebe. A better man might feel guilt over how well he knew her body. It wasn't entirely appropriate that he'd memorized the curves of a friend and former employee—but Heath hadn't earned his reputation by being appropriate.

He interrupted whatever Matt was saying. "I just saw Phoebe Mars. I should go say hi."

"Oh, right. She worked at Piri, didn't she?"

"Yeah. She was our pastry chef." Until Heath's business partner had talked her into quitting.

Selfish SOB. Cam had strung her along and cost Piri an award-winning pastry chef just because the jerk had thought it would be too awkward to work with her after they broke up. When Cam had dumped her, Heath had battled back an uncharacteristic urge to take a swing at his partner for breaking her heart. Tonight, his feelings were more conflicted. He didn't like the idea of Phoebe hurting, yet some part of him—a dark, disloyal part—delighted in her freedom.

Heath turned his attention back to Matt. "You have vermouth and green olives back there?" A moment later, he headed outside with his own drink and a vodka martini for Phoebe.

She stood alone, or as alone as one could be on a balcony with four other people, staring at the city skyline while the breeze toyed with the ends of her hair. She had gorgeous strawberry blonde hair that fell past her shoulder blades. When she worked in the kitchen, she secured it in a tight, low bun; Heath always savored these rare occasions when it tumbled free in riotous waves.

He joined her at the railing. June in Atlanta was steamy, enveloping him in heat, but even if it had been snowing outside, Phoebe in that dress would have raised his temperature. "I don't suppose you'd consider chugging whatever's left in that wineglass so I can look gallant by bringing you a fresh drink?"

"Heath!" Her full lips curved in a welcoming smile.

He only had a moment to admire the cleavage displayed by the plunging neckline before she threw her arms around him in an unexpectedly fierce hug. Her lush curves pressed against his body, and, damn, she smelled delicious. Was the scent perfume or just the by-product of working each day with cinnamon and vanilla and other tantalizing ingredients? He had the fleeting impulse to drop the glasses in his hands so he could hold her close, capture her mouth with his own and find out if she tasted equally delicious.

She pulled away, her smile sheepish. "Sorry. I almost knocked you over, didn't I?"

"You don't hear me complaining." He'd happily allow her to knock him flat on his back if he could convince her to join him.

"I was excited to see a friendly face."

He raised an eyebrow. She was hardly among strangers. When Bobbi had interviewed her as part of a dessert series last year, they'd become instant friends. Phoebe probably knew half the people here.

"A *single* friendly face," she added. "It's nice not to be the only one without a date. Or are you here with someone?" She gazed past him into the condo, her whiskey-gold eyes searching.

"Nope, I'm alone." He thanked his lucky stars that the flight attendant he'd originally asked to come with him was somewhere over the Midwest right now. "I have it on good authority that the Kemp sisters are also solo—and on the prowl. Protect me from them?"

"Oh, please. You haven't needed anyone's help handling women a day in your life."

Not since college anyway. Regardless, it wasn't either of the Kemp sisters he wanted to handle.

Phoebe set her wineglass on the patio table. "I'm not finishing that. The floral notes are overpowering, and life's too short to drink mediocre wine. What did you bring me?"

"Vodka martini, two olives, splash of brine." He winked at her. "I know you like it dirty."

Color tinged her cheeks, but she grinned back at him. "Yum." Phoebe was an interesting contrast. Although she blushed at his habitual teasing, she'd often been the first to laugh if someone made a ribald joke in the kitchen. Muffled laughter, but Heath heard it just the same.

As she took the martini glass, her fingers brushed his. A rush of desire went through him, surprising him with its intensity. When she'd worked at Piri, they'd bumped and jostled each other plenty of times in a crowded kitchen.

But she hadn't been single then.

"You look amazing tonight." His gaze dropped to the creamy swells of her breasts for a moment before he made himself meet her eyes again. "Different, but amazing."

"I can't take credit for that. It's easy to look amazing when your roommate's professionally trained to make people look good. Gwen is responsible for my wardrobe, my cosmetics and my hair—not to mention making me attend the party."

"She talked you into rearranging your schedule?" He and Gwen didn't particularly get along, not since a disastrous double date Phoebe had engineered, but he appreciated that the woman had convinced Phoebe to be here.

"More like she rearranged my schedule for me. She called James, who is the nicest boss ever. No offense."

He grinned. "None taken." *Nice* wasn't one of the adjectives that described him.

"I'm glad they persuaded me. I would have hated to miss Bobbi's birthday. I was just clinging to the excuse of work because—" Her eyes widened, locking on a point behind Heath. Her fair complexion paled beyond its normal ivory.

Damn. Heath didn't need to turn around to know Cam was inside. Probably with a date, judging from Phoebe's pained expression. It had been too much to hope that her attending the party looking like fantasy made flesh was a sign she'd moved past her feelings for the hotshot chef. They'd been together for years. She wasn't shallow enough to put that behind her in a matter of days.

"Phoebe?" He took her drink and set both their glasses on the nearby railing. "Do you trust me?"

Her gaze snapped back to his. "Sure."

That makes one of us. Heath knew better than to trust his own motives as he cupped the side of her face. Helping her salvage her dignity provided an excellent excuse to touch her, and being successful in business had taught him a thing or two about seizing opportunities. Tendrils of her fiery hair tickled his arm as he leaned closer. "I have a plan."

Then he pulled her tight against him and kissed her.

2

THE WORLD SPUN wildly around Phoebe as her brain tried to process what was happening. Her body, meanwhile, just wanted to revel in Heath's kiss. He traced her lips, and then his tongue met hers, the hint of bourbon a sweet burn that spread through her. His hands were at the small of her back, holding her against him in a way that gave her a whole new appreciation for his body. She'd always considered him a sharp dresser, but suddenly she wondered what he'd look like without the well-tailored suits.

He kissed with assertive confidence, like a man who knew exactly what she wanted and was happy to give it to her.

For the past ten days, she'd been like a sleepwalker, cocooned in dull numbness. She hadn't even realized how detached she'd been until now, with sensation rushing through her. Her skin tingled with pleasure. She angled her head, encouraging Heath to deepen the kiss. He did, and a shock wave of desire hit her. When was the last time she'd felt this damn good?

She curled her fingers in his dark hair. It was thick and soft, free of the stiff styling products that Cam—

Oh, God. *Cam*.

The memory of her ex's presence jolted her from the sensual daze, and she staggered back, glad for the support of the iron-and-concrete railing behind her. "What the hell was that?" she asked, her voice little more than a breathless whisper.

Unreadable emotion flashed in Heath's green eyes. Regret? Before he could answer, a guy from the far end of the balcony whistled at them. "We were debating whether we'd have to throw a bucket of water on you guys. Guess you two don't need a party to have a good time."

Cheeks stinging with embarrassment, Phoebe retreated inside…but drew up short when she found herself face-to-face with a scowling Cam. Heath was instantly at her side, his hand pressed lightly to her spine. She couldn't tell if the gesture was meant to be comforting or possessive. But after the way every nerve in her body had just responded to him, the touch was like a brand through her beaded dress, as if her entire universe had contracted to his palm and fingers. For a second, she couldn't even register what Cam was saying. She simply held her breath, waiting to see how Heath touched her next.

"—you two would be here together." Cam's words, at first just a meaningless buzz, slowly took shape. He'd pasted a smile on his face, the polite one he forced himself to use with important food critics he didn't like, but anger edged his tone.

"Phoebe isn't technically my date," Heath said. "I'm just grateful I ran into her. You never know where a chance encounter might lead." He looked at her when he said it, his tone meaningful.

Her breath hitched before sanity caught up to her. Heath was deliberately baiting his own business partner, making Cam think there was something between them. Why would he do that? The two men were planning to open a second restaurant together, and that process would run a lot smoother without any manufactured tension between them.

Cam looked startled by Heath's insinuation. "I, ah…" His gaze went to Phoebe, searching, and she tried to look cheerful, not at all like she'd rather be home in yoga pants than facing her ex. Then his date cleared her throat. "Oh! Allow me to introduce you to Donna Moore."

"Dana," the blonde snapped, her eyes narrowing in displeasure.

"Dana. Of course. That's what I meant to say. Dana, this is Heath and Phoebe."

"Charmed." If her tone was any icier, they could use it to make frozen drinks.

"How about we, uh, go wish Bobbi a happy birthday?" Cam suggested, steering his date away. As they merged into the crowd, he cast one final glance over his shoulder.

At me. Phoebe fought a grin at the surprising knowledge that he was jealous. As the executive chef of a noted restaurant, Cam was often in the spotlight, giving interviews and emerging from the kitchen to greet special customers. She'd been so proud of him, content to bake her desserts and watch him soak up the accolades. But it was a refreshing change to be the one getting a little attention.

Belatedly, she recalled Heath's words before his mouth claimed hers. *I have a plan.* Understanding dawned. "You kissed me to make him jealous."

"Hope you don't think that's too petty or juvenile."

"Actually…" She recalled the times Cam had praised her as his muse and led her to believe marriage was in their distant future, contrasting those moments with the brutal shock of his announcement that they were "stifling" each other. He hadn't even had the balls to make a clean break. Instead, he'd suggested they still go out occasionally—which she'd translated as code for wanting a backup sexual partner on the nights nothing better came along. *Hell, no.* "That was awesome."

She just wished she'd realized sooner that Heath's kiss was only playacting. As she recalled the greedy way she'd clutched at him and how her toes had curled inside Gwen's borrowed stilettos, embarrassment rippled through her. *Way to come on like a sex-starved hussy.* She deeply regretted the loss of the martini she'd left behind.

"Thank you," she told him. "But you didn't have to do that."

"Kissing a beautiful woman is no hardship."

Heath thinks I'm beautiful. There was a momentary flush of giddiness before she reminded herself that he was a connoisseur of women. He appreciated many forms and shapes, the way she could savor dozens of desserts from around the world without ever picking a favorite. How many countless women had she heard him call "sweetheart" or "gorgeous"? His compliment, though flattering, wasn't personal.

"Besides," he added, frowning in Cam's direction, "the big jerk had it coming. You were the best thing that ever happened to him."

"That's what Gwen said, too." She was blessed to have such loyal friends, even ones who inexplicably disliked each other. The day Cam had broken up with her, Gwen had partially blamed Heath.

"That business partner makes single life look so glamorous, with his endless parade of women," her friend had said. "Cam got so distracted by what he can't have that he took you for granted." Phoebe didn't fault Heath, but the "grass is greener" explanation made as much sense as anything else. She'd thought they were happy.

"He is going to regret losing you," Heath said. "If he thinks you've found someone, it might speed up his epiphany."

Found someone? As in, an actual relationship and not just a quick kiss at a party? "You aren't suggesting we make him think that you and I are dating?"

"That's exactly what I'm suggesting."

She laughed nervously. "No offense, but who would buy that? You're never seen with the same woman twice." Oddly, few of his ex-lovers seemed bitter. Most continued to smile and sigh when they saw him. *He must be* really *good in bed.* She felt wicked, secretly speculating on his sexual performance while he stood there giving her relationship advice.

The corner of Heath's mouth curled in a half grin that made her immediately reevaluate her last thought. This man could teach a master's class in wickedness. Next to him, she was a total novice.

"Why stop at making him think we're 'dating'?" he asked. "You want to really get under his skin, let him think we're having a scorching affair hotter than an Atlanta heat wave. As for no one believing us..." His gaze arrested hers, and he shifted closer. She could almost feel the hard planes of his body through the fabric of her dress. "You'd be surprised at how convincing I can be."

Oh, Lord, did she need a drink. Not her martini—ice water. Her throat had gone dry, and the crowded room was stifling. "I don't know."

Though she didn't doubt Heath's persuasive skills, she herself was a terrible liar. And she was still sorting through the aftermath of her breakup. Did she *want* to win back Cam's affection? She was furious with him, but there were good memories and years of emotional investment. Either way, her feminine pride had taken a hit when he'd dumped her. Having Heath look at her as if he wanted to lick dark chocolate ganache off her bare skin was heady, yet confusing.

He rocked back on his heels, symbolically restoring the platonic distance between them. "Completely up to you," he said. "Think about it, and we'll talk soon. Now, if you'll excuse me, I should flee. There's a Kemp sister heading this way."

She chuckled, but he raised an interesting point about other women. "Heath, if people think you and I are a couple, won't it hinder your love life?"

"Sacrifice I'm willing to make." He grinned. "Temporarily. I've actually been swamped with work stuff recently and had to reschedule my last two attempted dates. So contrary to my suave reputation, I *can* go a couple of weeks without a woman on my arm."

"Still, it seems pretty one-sided, me using you to make Cam jealous."

"I'm at your disposal. Use me any way you want."

It was the kind of outrageously flirtatious comment he routinely made. She knew better than to read anything serious into it. *He's a buddy*, she reminded herself. *He's not genuinely propositioning you*.

Yeah, she knew that. Intellectually. But the reminder would have been a lot more convincing without the memory of that scalding kiss still buzzing through her system.

"WHAT DO YOU mean Heath kissed you last night?" Gwen went from lazily lounging on the sofa to bolt upright and hyperalert—or as alert as one could look with bed head and flying toaster pajamas. She sounded scandalized, which was ironic considering the details of her own personal life.

Grinning at her friend's reaction, Phoebe put her

empty coffee cup in the sink. Then she made a bee-line for her favorite armchair, the first piece of non–garage sale furniture she'd purchased after starting her side business of wedding cakes. Their apartment was modest, but the kitchen met her picky specifications.

"Which part of kissing don't you understand?" she joked. "His lips, my lips. After the sordid tales of you and the hot stunt guy, I *know* you're familiar with the concept."

Gwen scowled, clearly not amused.

Wow, she really doesn't approve of Heath. Not for the first time, Phoebe wished that two of her favorite people could get along better. She'd attempted to fix them up last year, thinking they had a lot in common, but the double date with her and Cam had been a massive failure. Even before Gwen's blasphemous declaration that baseball was boring, Heath hadn't been his usual charming self. He'd seemed oddly distracted. "Look, it wasn't a real kiss. Heath wanted to help me make Cam jealous and offered to let me use him."

A flutter of guilty pleasure went through her. What might a woman do with Heath Jensen entirely under her control?

Gwen shook her head firmly. "You don't want any part of that. Making sure your ex sees you looking hot is one thing, but mind games are beneath you."

"Maybe." She recalled Cam's stricken expression after he'd seen Heath kiss her and her vindictive delight. *Maybe not.* "But it's not like you to judge.

You're the one always encouraging me to be reckless, have an adventure."

"Yeah, but I figured you'd start small and work your way up. When a person goes skiing for the first time, she doesn't head straight for the black diamond trails. She starts with the bunny slopes! Heath is no bunny."

"I know the two of you didn't exactly hit it off, but Heath would never hurt me."

"Not intentionally," Gwen agreed. "But you would be in way over your head trying to fake a red-hot fling with him. Next to that borderline man-whore, you're a nun."

"I went out last night in a dress cut down to my navel. I am *not* a nun."

"Okay, wrong choice of word. But you have to admit you're not…" Gwen peered at her with a combination of affection and sympathy. "Like when you talked about your love life with Cam? It sounded comfortable, maybe even a little routine."

"Maybe I've never had a quickie with a ripped stuntman in a makeup trailer, but our sex life was plenty satisfactory!" Oh, there was a ringing endorsement. *Hey, baby, wanna get satisfactory?* Was that why Cam had left her—because the sex had been boring?

After growing up with a mother who'd done everything she could to impress on her that sex was evil, Phoebe had congratulated herself more than once on not turning out to be phobic. Still, her love life was pretty conventional. There'd been the boyfriend her freshman year in college who'd been as inexperienced as she was. He'd treated her like a princess, but the sex had not been earth-shaking. Then there'd been the bartender she'd dated during her year of working at a bakery. On the nights he worked, he didn't get home until almost 3:00 a.m., and her predawn shift had started at four. Their sex life had been great... when they were both awake at the same time. Cam was by far the best lover she'd ever had, but now she realized she didn't have much basis for comparison.

If she'd been more inventive in bed, would she have held his interest longer?

That was a depressing thought.

Phoebe sighed. "I guess instead of making fun of those Weird Ways to Bring Him to His Knees articles in your fashion magazines, I should be studying them for advice." Then again, why read generic tips written by another woman? Why not get a guy's opinion? She snapped her fingers. "Or Heath could help me."

"What? Let's not do anything hasty."

"Heath offered to help." *Use me any way you want.* "Why not take him up on it?" The more she thought about it, the more sense it made. "Best-case scenario, I win back the man I was planning to spend my life with, after an appropriate period of groveling. Worst case, Cam and I stay split up, but I salvage my pride by making sure he knows I'm not wasting away *and* I pick up tips on being more seductive. Where's the bad?"

"In Heath Jensen's arms," Gwen said darkly.

There, her roommate was wrong. Because being

kissed by Heath had been very, very good. And that had only been a brief preview of his expertise. Her pulse quickened.

How much more of Heath's sensual skill would she experience firsthand? She glanced across the room to where her phone was charging.

Only one way to find out.

3

ARMS AND BACK muscles straining, a bead of sweat trickling down his chest, Heath raised himself into his last set of pull-ups. It was tempting to use the buzzing cell phone on the nightstand as an excuse to quit the workout, but after starting high school as the shortest, chunkiest guy in the freshman class, he took his athletic regimen seriously. Staying in shape required effort, especially for someone who worked with—and enjoyed the hell out of—food. He glanced down at the phone. Unless it was someone from the restaurant, and therefore a potential emergency, he'd call whoever it was back.

But then he saw Phoebe's name on the screen, and he almost lost his grip on the bar.

Dropping to his feet, he snatched up the phone. "Hello?" *So I'll do an extra set of reps tomorrow.* No big deal.

"Hey." Her voice was soft, tentative. "Did I catch you at a bad time?"

That depended. Was she calling to tell him she didn't appreciate his meddling last night and that he'd better keep his hands to himself? "Just finishing up a workout." He reached for his bottle of water. "What can I do for you?"

"Teach me to be sexy."

Thank God he hadn't opened the water yet. An announcement like that would have had him spluttering. His obituary in the *AJC* would read Restaurateur Drowns in Bedroom.

"Phoebe. Not to state the obvious, but you are sexy."

"The word people use is *cute.*"

Stupid people, maybe. Not even a chef's jacket and apron could hide those curves. And anyone who paid close enough attention to her mischievous smile would discover an alluring potential to misbehave. How did people miss it? Hell, he'd been trying to *un*see it for months.

Maybe now he didn't have to. For the moment, she was unattached. And he was no longer her employer.

"It's not like I suffer from low self-esteem," she said matter-of-factly. "I'm attractive, and I'm talented in the kitchen. But I'm not...you know. Va va voom."

"Did you not look in a mirror before you left the house last night?" For that matter, was she oblivious to how aroused he'd been when she kissed him back? He got hard every time he remembered the taste of her mouth beneath his, the feel of her fingers in his hair as she tugged him closer.

"Eye makeup and a low-cut dress are superficial

window dressing. I want a more meaningful make-over. I want to be exciting." She lowered her voice. "Seductive."

A more seductive Phoebe. God help him.

"If I take Cam back," she continued, "I don't want to worry that I'm not enough to hold his interest."

Cam. Right.

Heath had been so busy picturing Phoebe as a confident seductress that he'd momentarily forgotten this was all to prove a point to her ex. *Which was* your *idea, genius.* He could hardly fault her for taking him at his word. Hadn't he offered to help in whatever way she needed? She was, after all, one of his best friends.

"You suggested we pretend to be dating," she said, "and I thought that while we're spending some extra time together, maybe you could give me pointers."

It was like the lamb asking the wolf to help make her more delicious. The noble part of him truly wanted to help her; the other 99 percent of him was preoccupied by the possibilities. For months, working alongside her, he'd been a gentleman—or, at least, his version of one. There'd been some playfully naughty banter, but he'd kept his hands to himself. And now she wanted to put herself in his hands and have him teach her about sex?

If he was a better person, he'd warn her away. "Are you free for dinner?"

"T-tonight?" The way she stumbled over the word made him wonder if she was already rethinking her request, or if she was just surprised he'd agreed.

"Yeah. I—" Reality caught up to him. He couldn't

Tanya Michaels 33

miss work tonight. They were hosting some celebs in town to shoot a movie. He wanted to personally ensure that everything went smoothly and that service was stellar. As hard as he'd worked to make Piri successful, he had no intentions of slacking off now. They needed the extra profits to help bankroll a sister restaurant. "Wait, tonight's no good."

"Not for me, either. Sundays aren't as busy as Thursday through Saturday, when we have the dueling pianos, but the weekly wine tastings are growing in popularity. I've got an entire dessert menu pairing chocolate and red wine."

"What about tomorrow?"

"That could work. I go in on Mondays, but after I get the desserts prepped, I can probably leave. It's our quietest night. Or if you want to wait a little longer, I have Tuesdays and Wednesdays off."

No, he emphatically did not want to wait. Part of him was still tempted to talk her into calling in sick and coming over tonight. Before she came to her senses. "Then, I'll cook you dinner tomorrow. It can be after eight if you need to help with the dinner rush." By nature, he was a night person, and working in the restaurant industry had amplified that.

"Or you could come to my apartment and I can cook," she offered. "I owe you. After all, *you're* doing *me* the favor."

Debatable. "If I come over, can you guarantee my safety? That roommate of yours would probably stab me with a salad fork the first chance she got."

"Good point. At your place, we won't be interrupted."

Private seduction lessons with Phoebe.

He couldn't have imagined a better fantasy if he'd tried. And he had a *very* active imagination.

"UM..." AMY HUANG, the apprentice chef, darted a nervous glance at Phoebe and then looked back at the crystallized mess that was supposed to have been caramel sauce.

Dammit. Earlier, the top of a limoncello sponge cake had collapsed, now this. Embarrassment prickled along Phoebe's skin, and her fingers clenched around the handle of the pan. She was supposed to be teaching Amy, not demonstrating a showcase of what-not-to-dos.

"Guess everything they say about Mondays is true," Phoebe said lightly, trying to contain the annoyance she felt over her mistakes. "Why don't you take a quick break and I'll clean up?"

Amy's expression was dubious. "I don't think James hired you to do dishes."

"If you want to get technical, he didn't hire me to ruin perfectly good caramel, either."

At that, the apprentice chef laughed. "Well, I would appreciate a few minutes to call my boyfriend. He's out of town celebrating his birthday with his brothers."

"Go." Phoebe waved her away, trying not to succumb to a moment of cynicism. Was Amy's boyfriend missing her, or eyeing other prospects? Were his brothers the type of guys who would respect a commitment, or the type who would try to convince the birthday boy that what Amy didn't know wouldn't hurt her?

Not all men were heartless liars, she reminded herself. Take Heath, for example. He might date dozens of women, but she couldn't imagine him deceiving one. He made no secret that he liked to have a good time—but there was more to him than that. He was an ambitious worker and a devoted friend. She was still a little surprised he'd agreed to put his own love life on hiatus to help her.

Surprised and nervous.

She wasn't sure what to expect when she had dinner with him tonight, which probably explained the atypical mistakes she was making. She'd been distracted since she got here. *Who are you kidding?* She'd been distracted since she'd hung up the phone with him yesterday. The way his low voice had rumbled "you are sexy" had wound its way through her, as irresistible as the aroma of apple-cinnamon cake in the oven.

"Hey, there." James joined her at the industrial sink. Of Norwegian descent, the big blond man was a cross between a Viking and teddy bear. From the concerned look on his face, it was clear he'd heard about her mishaps. She hated to fail him after he'd campaigned so long to hire her.

Despite the many times they'd joked about him stealing her away from Piri, she'd never once thought she would have to take him up on his offer of a job.

She'd believed she and Cam were a lasting team—personally *and* professionally. *Wrong on both counts.*

It would take a long time to establish the same kind of rhythm with this kitchen staff that she'd enjoyed at Piri, but she loved James's upscale bar and his infectious enthusiasm. Besides, she needed this job. Her side business in wedding cake orders and other specialty items was growing steadily, but it was nowhere near a full-time income.

"You want to head out a little early tonight?" James offered.

"Trying to get rid of me before I burn the place down?"

"Hell, yes. You're only supposed to resort to arson for insurance when the business *isn't* turning a profit. We're actually succeeding."

"No surprise there," she said fondly. "Good concept, good location, great management." The tapas plates were wonderful, and now that Phoebe was on board, the dessert selection of tasty traditional choices, like cheesecake and peach cobbler, also featured more creative dishes inspired by sweet liqueurs and cocktails.

Throughout the week, the bar offered something for everyone—from open-mic nights to the engaging "dueling pianists," including James's longtime boyfriend, to last night's wine tasting, which paired vintages with bite-size appetizers designed to highlight the notes. A newly engaged couple had come in to celebrate with friends and toast their happiness. Phoebe had rolled out a special cake for them and, after witnessing how in love they were, it had been a struggle not to cry in the crepe batter when she'd returned to the kitchen.

"Don't beat yourself up for having an off night," James advised. "Gwen and I shouldn't have bullied you into seeing Cam at that birthday party. It must have been awful. If Steve and I ever—" He broke off, wincing. "I can't even think about that."

"Me, neither. You guys are perfect together." Then again, what did she know? There'd been a time when she'd believed that about her and Cameron, too. The pain of getting dumped was two-tiered, like the coconut wedding cake she was baking this week. First, there was the obvious pain of rejection and loss. But beneath that was a nagging feeling of stupidity, the questioning why she hadn't seen it coming. She was starting to second-guess her own judgment.

Any more pastry catastrophes tonight and she might start to second-guess her culinary skills, too.

She sighed. "You know what? I will leave a little bit early. I have plans later anyway." At the thought of what those plans entailed, her face heated. Part of her still couldn't believe she'd followed through on her impulse to ask Heath for his help. But the request had been over the phone, from a safe distance. What would it be like to actually face him tonight? Nothing embarrassed the man, so there was no telling how explicit his pointers might be.

No problem, you've had years of experience with Gwen's outrageous bluntness. True, but Gwen didn't have Heath's green eyes, or a deep voice that was as addictive as hazelnut truffles. And Phoebe wasn't even going to think about his mouth or the way he kissed, like he knew all a woman's secrets.

James gave a low whistle under his breath. "Wow, these must be some very rowdy after-hours plans for you to look that guilty. I take it Gwen has schemed something to cheer you up?"

She bit the inside of her cheek, trying not to dwell on her roommate's dire warnings. "Nothing like that. I'm just grabbing a late dinner with Heath."

"Heath Jensen? Nice." He bumped her shoulder with his own. "But I'm a little miffed you haven't mentioned until now that something's going on."

An automatic protest sprang to her lips, but she stopped herself from assuring him that she and Heath were platonic buddies. After all, the plan was for people to think there was something between the two of them, right? "I ran into him at the party Saturday," she said. "And our encounter took a…surprising turn. I didn't say anything because I'm not sure what will happen yet."

James's pale blue eyes twinkled. "Well, go find out."

As THE ELEVATOR slowly made the climb to what Heath jokingly called his seventh-floor penthouse, Phoebe tried to ignore the mirrored doors. Even though she'd changed out of her kitchen uniform of double-breasted jacket, elastic-waisted dark pants and pin-striped baker's cap, no one was going to mistake her for a femme fatale. Her face, devoid of makeup, was still flushed from hours in a hot kitchen, and her loose bun was trying to escape its confines via frizz. The black skirt with dark metallic polka dots was cute, although a conservative length that stopped just above her knees; the loose blouse she wore over a copper-colored tank top was mostly shapeless. And her flat scandals screamed *sensible*.

As the doors parted, panic flitted through her. A plan that had seemed almost reasonable yesterday morning suddenly seemed insane. How could anyone make *her* a seductress? Gwen was right. *This is a huge mistake.*

Embarrassment churning in her stomach, she almost turned to go. She could call Heath from her car and tell him something had come up—work, or a headache, or alien abduction. *But aren't you sick of always trying so hard to avoid mistakes?*

She'd spent the better part of her adolescence feeling like she *was* a mistake. Her mother certainly hadn't planned to get pregnant as a teenager. The woman's constant dire warnings, intended to keep her daughter from repeating her bad choices, had left Phoebe terrified of doing anything wrong. Phoebe had wanted to be the perfect daughter, to atone for her existence. And hadn't she tried to be the perfect girlfriend to Cam? That sure as hell hadn't gotten her anywhere. Anger heated her skin, and she ripped the blouse that suddenly felt claustrophobic over her head, shoving it into her shoulder bag.

Every time she put a dessert in the oven, she hoped it would turn out perfectly. But sometimes soufflés fell and crème brûlée torches led to fire extinguishers. Was that a reason to stop cooking?

The door swung open, startling her from her thoughts. Heath stood barefoot in a pair of dark slacks, his royal blue shirt untucked and rolled up at the sleeves. "I thought I heard the elevator." He raised an eyebrow at her. "Are you planning to come inside?"

She lifted her chin. To hell with being afraid—maybe it was time to start making some mistakes. "You bet your ass I am."

4

HEATH STEPPED ASIDE to let in Phoebe, assessing her mood. He'd heard the elevator in the hall ding almost five minutes ago, but no knock had followed. He'd assumed that meant Phoebe was having second thoughts, yet there wasn't a trace of hesitation in her body language as she marched into the loft, her posture regal and her shapely arms displayed to full advantage by a silky tank top.

His apartment often impressed his dates. This would be when the oohs and aahs took place. Phoebe, however, had been here a dozen times. She didn't gush over the skyline view through the floor-to-ceiling window or the gleaming hardwood floors or the blown-glass sculptures that added splashes of vibrant color against the white leather furniture. Instead, she closed her eyes and inhaled deeply—Heath couldn't help noticing the rise and fall of her breasts beneath her top.

"Mmm. I love the smell of fresh basil."

"Hope you like the way it tastes, too." He led her to the kitchen, which was separated from the living room only by a marble-topped counter. "My plan is to sear scallops and serve them alla caprese."

Taking a seat atop one of the bar stools, she sighed happily. "It's so decadent having someone cook for me. When you're a chef, you're used to doing the food preparation, not just at work but for family and friends."

"Cam's an executive chef. Didn't he cook for you?" The question was an automatic response to her words, but he regretted asking. The last thing he'd intended was to bring up the guy who'd jilted her, not when she was looking so relaxed and happy.

"Frequently. But it was…" She paused, considering. "When he had me try new dishes, it was a matter of wanting my professional opinion on how to make his creation better. He called me his muse. It sounded romantic," she said in a small voice. "But maybe it was just a glorified term for *taste tester*."

For a second, Heath hated his business partner almost as much as he hated the self-doubt on Phoebe's face. "Well, I don't have any 'creations' I need to perfect. All I have is a limited culinary repertoire I use in a feeble attempt to impress women who turn me on." He reached across the counter, tipping her chin up with his finger. "Gorgeous redheads, for instance, who kiss like pagan goddesses."

She blinked at that, but then shook her head. "Laying it on a little thick, aren't you?"

"Have you met me? I have no shame. I do, however, have excellent taste in wine. Can I pour you some of the pinot gris I have chilled?"

"Yes, please. In a really large glass."

"Thirsty? Or nervous?"

"Trying to drown out my roommate's voice in my head. Gwen thinks this is a terrible idea, my asking for your help."

"Just because you asked doesn't mean you're committed to accepting it. You can leave anytime." The words scraped against his throat—he wanted her here—but he made himself voice the disclaimer. He was willing to take advantage of the situation that had presented itself, but he didn't want to take advantage of *her.*

"I know." Her eyes locked with his.

Did she feel the same blast of heat that surged through him? The cold bottle of wine was a welcome respite. He poured two glasses, obligingly filling hers almost to the rim.

"Thank you," she said softly. "Not just for the wine or dinner, but for all of this. It's not like I can make Cam jealous by myself, right?"

"So you've decided you definitely want to win him back?" He reached for one of the skillets hanging over the kitchen island and smacked it down on the burner.

"I don't know. My emotions are all jumbled up. But there was a married couple who came into the bar last week to celebrate their tenth anniversary—the man had the pianists serenade his wife with a song from their wedding. When I see people like that, part of me still imagines me and Cam ten or fifteen years from now. I thought he was my future." She sipped her wine. "I suppose you never think about the future."

"Sure I do. All the time." He turned on the gas burner, then poured olive oil into the skillet. "Most of my waking hours lately have been spent thinking about scouting restaurant locations in Miami." He'd made some excellent contacts over the past few years attending the South Beach Food and Wine Festival, and he'd identified several flourishing neighborhoods that might be a good fit for his and Cam's second venture.

"I meant a romantic future," Phoebe said. "Do you think you'll ever want more than hot one-night stands?"

"Some of those are hot *weekends*. I can go longer than a single night."

For a change, she didn't blush at his teasing. Instead, she wagged her finger at him. "You aren't as shallow as you let people believe."

"Wanna bet?"

There was a stubborn glint in her eye, but rather than argue, she took another sip of her drink. "Maybe I spend too much time trying to plan for the future. Gwen thinks I need to live in the moment and…have adventures."

He grinned. "What kind of adventures?" Knowing her roommate, Gwen wasn't suggesting scuba diving or hot-air-balloon rides. *Sex on a hot-air balloon, maybe.*

Now Phoebe did blush, a rosy stain spreading across her face. She glanced past him at the stove, where oil hissed and sizzled in the pan. "You should turn down the heat."

He obligingly flicked the control knob before adding the scallops. "I thought our purpose was to turn *up* the heat. You wanted to know if you could be more seductive, right? Exciting?" Those had been her exact words. Heath had the sudden urge to offer her all the excitement she could handle. "What's the most exciting sexual thing you've done?"

"Lose my virginity? Although *exciting* isn't the first adjective I'd pick to describe that encounter." Frustration pinched her expression. "People like you and Gwen don't get it—some of us *aren't* exciting. That's why I'm here."

If her love life hadn't been exhilarating enough, then her sexual partners were also to blame. But he didn't point that out, not wanting to reintroduce Cam in the conversation. "All right, what adventurous things have you *thought* about doing? 'Fess up. If you didn't have a wicked streak, you wouldn't have sought my help."

"I guess that's true." After a moment's consideration, her lips curved in a small secret smile that left him hard. It was the naughtiest expression he'd ever seen on her face, a glimpse at the mischievous Phoebe he'd known was there but who was seldom allowed to come out and play. Damn, she was sexy. If Heath's shirt hadn't been untucked, the situation might be embarrassing.

"Phoebe Mars. What dirty thing are you imagining?" *And are you in need of a volunteer?*

"When Gwen and I first moved into our apartment, back before I met Ca—back when I was single," she amended, "we lived across from a guy who worked at a local gym. He was so toned." She paused for a moment, appreciating the memory. "Anyway, my desk is pushed up against my bedroom window—almost blocking it, but not completely. I was searching recipes on the computer and when I glanced up, I realized his blinds were partially open. He was undressing in his room, and he was, um, erect."

Yeah, there was a lot of that going around.

"Before he disappeared from view, I saw him reach down and grip his erection." Her breathing was audible, her face flushed.

"And you wanted to watch him get off?"

"No—well, maybe," she reflected. "But for a second, I thought he might have seen me through the window and my imagination ran wild. I imagined *him* catching *me* naked. Imagined what it would be like for him to watch me…touch myself."

Working in a kitchen required being good with one's hands. Heath had seen her knead and stir and frost countless times. Now his gaze flew to those talented hands, and he was assailed by the erotic image of her fingers cupped over the red-gold curls between her thighs, furiously working her sex. Or would she take her time with leisurely caresses, drawing out her pleasure? He'd thought he was hard *before*? His dick was like steel.

She bit her lip, and he tried not to imagine the

scrape of her teeth across his skin. "I shocked you, didn't I?"

Hell, yes. In the best possible way. "Of course not. This is me. I'm unshockable."

"Really?"

"It's not uncommon to have exhibitionist or voyeurism fantasies." He would be having several later tonight.

Her expression brightened with so much joy that one would think she'd just been named the ACF Pastry Chef of the Year. "Thank you."

"Anytime. But I'm not sure what I did to deserve gratitude."

She looked down, concentrating on her wineglass rather than meeting his gaze. "My mom got pregnant as a teen, and she worked really hard to make sure that never happened to me. Most of my life, I was half convinced *kissing* was evil, never mind fantasies about..."

"Masturbating in front of a sexy stranger?"

The blunt words heightened the color in her cheeks, but she nodded. "You're a relief to be around. I mean, you're cocky and frequently a pain in the ass—"

"Guilty."

"But you aren't judgmental and I don't constantly worry that I'm going to disappoint you. You're a good friend, Heath."

A better friend would help her win back the man she loved without picturing her naked. "No, I'm a selfish hedonist. But the benefit of having no shame is that I don't let it bother me."

Her lips twitched, and she raised her glass. "To shameless pleasure."

"I'll drink to that."

PHOEBE LEANED BACK against the cool leather of the couch, her feet tucked beneath her while her sandals lay askew on the floor. Dinner had been yummy and their discussion hadn't been quite as charged as she'd feared. After what she'd revealed earlier, she hadn't known what to expect and had experienced a moment of apprehension when they sat down together.

Almost as if sensing her nerves, Heath had kicked off an innocuous conversation about how they'd tweak the Braves lineup if they had the power to trade players. Later, when she'd brought up wanting to add some new savory pastries to James's menu, Heath had waggled his brows and teased her about experimentation. But, by Heath standards, he'd behaved. Now she was enjoying the nighttime view through the window while he washed dishes, which he'd insisted on doing himself. The city lights twinkled, combining with the two glasses of wine she'd had to make her feel utterly relaxed.

Liar.

If she were honest with herself, she'd acknowledge the buzz of awareness that crackled beneath the surface of mellow contentment. When Heath's green eyes landed on her or he moved close to refill her glass, it was *not* relaxing. She felt tense—not in the stressed-out, frazzled kind of way, but high-strung just the same. All her senses were on full alert, and her skin tingled. It was a reaction that had caught her off guard when she arrived earlier and continued to take her by surprise, even though one would think she'd have adjusted after the first time. But it was disorienting to react so strongly to *Heath*. Sure, he was attractive—maybe one of the best-looking men in Atlanta—but he always had been. They'd worked together for over a year and she'd never felt this way.

Of course, that had been before he kissed her. What had she told Gwen? That it hadn't been a real kiss? *Please. If that kiss had been any more real, you would have exploded in a fiery blaze of spontaneous combustion.*

Mentally and emotionally, Phoebe was in a vulnerable place right now, and she wasn't sure what she wanted. Physically, she was less ambivalent. Her body had responded to Heath's kiss with a swift, primal certainty she was having trouble forgetting. She drained the last of her wine, although what she probably needed was to splash some cold water on her face.

"Want any more wine?" Heath asked from the edge of the kitchen. Finished with the dishes, he padded into the living room, moving with deceptively lazy grace. Although he projected a carefree vibe, she'd seen him hustle on busy nights and bust his ass to fix disasters.

Like your love life?

"I'd better not," she said. "If I have a third glass, I'll have to sleep here on your sofa."

He sat next to her, his grin devilish. "My bed's more comfortable."

She kicked him in reprimand—or, more accurately, she nudged his thigh with her bare foot.

He captured her toes in his hand, and she tried to pull away, suddenly alarmed. She was so unbearably ticklish that even sitting through pedicures was torturous. After a short-lived tickle fight in college, which had ended abruptly when her shrieks had brought the RA running, she'd wondered if the reason her skin was so sensitive to touch was because she was so unaccustomed to being touched. There hadn't been a lot of hugs and kisses in her household.

But there was nothing ticklish about the way Heath cupped her foot and applied firm pressure on the arch. He rotated his thumb with just the right force, and she nearly moaned. Her job required hours of standing, and even though she was smart enough to wear practical shoes to work, her feet still got sore. This was heaven.

"You are so good at that," she breathed.

"Practice makes perfect."

Her eyes were closed, so she couldn't see his expression, but she heard the seductive smile in his voice, hinting at skills far beyond foot massage. The man's middle name was probably Innuendo. He could talk about menu fonts and find a way to turn it into temptation.

Swinging both of her feet to the ground, she sat forward. "How do you make it sound like you're thinking about sex all the time?"

"By thinking about sex all the time." He grinned.

"Well, and food. Sometimes I think about ways to incorporate the two."

"I'm serious. Women throw themselves at you." His appeal wasn't just limited to the opposite sex. People in general were drawn into his orbit, with Gwen being the exception that proved the rule. If Heath had been a waiter instead of the restaurant's managing partner, he'd make more tips than the rest of the staff combined. "You have—"

"Irresistible sex appeal? Raw animal magnetism?"

She rolled her eyes. "Charisma. Can that be taught?" *I need a charisma coach.*

He considered that. "I think it's more something you discover than learn. But I know for a fact it can be honed. What color's your bra?"

"Excuse me?" She crossed her arms over her chest as if he suddenly had X-ray vision.

"I'm going for a metaphor-type thing here. You want people to see you as an exciting seductress, right? The kind of woman who might wear, I don't know, red lace. Or leather bondage gear. But do you see yourself as that woman?"

"I…" Hearing the word *bondage* come out of Heath's mouth short-circuited too many neurons for her to immediately respond. Oh, the mental images! "Um. What was the question?"

He leaned close, his eyes glittering with humor and something more predatory. Her stomach clenched with the same anticipation she'd felt on every roller coaster Gwen had ever made her ride. She recognized the way her lungs tightened at the top of the hill—before the adrenaline-spiking, heart-clutching plunge over the edge.

His fingers stroked up her arm to her shoulder, the touch electric. "The question, Phoebe, was about your bra." Hooking his index finger beneath her tank top, he tugged on the slim bra strap beneath. Then he sat back with a nod. "Black cotton. Not a bad start."

She stood, feeling suddenly restless and defensive. "I'm sure you've had experience with *many* bras, but I don't think you can actually tell that much about me from—"

"It has nothing to do with *my* opinion. No judgment, remember? It's about your self-image. Charisma is confidence—or at least being able to fake confidence exceptionally well." Getting to his feet, he held out his hand. "Come with me."

"We're not going lingerie shopping, are we?" Most stores would be closed, but there was always online retail. Besides, she'd bet next month's rent that he could charm a female manager into keeping a store open late for him.

"No. Although, if you want an expert opinion the next time you—*ow*." He made a show of rubbing his ribs where she'd jabbed him. "Was that really necessary?"

She gave him a sunny smile. "It really was."

"Brute." He walked to the opposite side of the room and at first she thought he was heading down the hallway. Toward his bedroom?

Her heart fluttered wildly, and she couldn't pin down whether the reaction was panic that Heath might make a move on her, or hopeful excitement. She knew he would never try to talk her in to something she didn't want to do. The problem was, she didn't know *what* she wanted. A wicked inner voice whispered, *Rebound fling.* Wasn't that a time-honored response to breakups? But flinging with a longtime friend— one who was Cam's business partner, no less—would be fraught with complications she didn't need.

Then she realized Heath wasn't going into the hall. He'd stopped in front of a large oval mirror in a gold-leaf frame that hung in the corner of the living room.

She raised an eyebrow. "Full-length mirror in the living room. Narcissism?"

He laughed. "Good feng shui, supposedly. It was a gift from an interior decorator I briefly dated."

Naturally. If Phoebe had a dollar for every woman he'd "briefly dated," she could open her own bakery in Paris.

Motioning her closer to the mirror, he changed the subject. "Did I tell you I'm one of this year's Over-Under honorees?"

It was an annual list of five people in the city's restaurant industry playfully deemed "overachievers under thirty."

"No! I can't believe you haven't mentioned it until now." She was thrilled for him, but a little embarrassed they'd spent so much time on her issues that it hadn't come up. "Congratulations, that's fantastic news."

He hitched one shoulder in an uncharacteristically modest shrug. "I appreciate the free publicity for Piri, but this award has always felt a bit like a popularity contest. It's not the most valid recognition out there."

"Of course *you're* blasé about popularity contests," she teased. "You've probably been winning them since kindergarten."

"Ha! Shows what you know. I—" He frowned. His abrupt halt was unlike him. In the event that he lost his train of thought, he was usually smooth enough to cover it.

"You what?" she prompted.

He flashed a brief smile. "I've been winning them since preschool. Now focus." His hands settled on her hips all too briefly as he slid her to his right so that she took up most of their shared reflection. "The reason I brought up being an honoree was because I wanted to tell you about the beautiful woman I'm asking to the awards luncheon."

"Oh." Disappointment left a sour taste in her mouth—so much for his being willing to curtail his romantic activities long enough to let people think *they* were dating.

He tapped a finger against her forehead. "*You*, Mars. Take a look and tell me I wouldn't be the luckiest guy there if you went with me."

His words melted away the disappointment, yet left a tiny kernel of guilt in its place. Despite his dismissive comment about popularity contests, the Over-Under luncheon was considered prestigious in their community. He should take a real date, not just someone trying to make an ex jealous. Her gaze flew to his. "Are you sure you—"

"How did you manage culinary school? You don't follow instructions." He stepped behind her, cupping her shoulders and turning her back toward the mirror. "You're supposed to be looking there."

"I feel silly." That was only half true. When she concentrated on her reflection, like she was supposed to be chanting a mantra of "I'm good enough, I'm pretty enough," she did indeed feel silly. But when she concentrated on how close Heath was standing, on how good he smelled and the warmth of his strong fingers curving over her bare skin...her pulse quickened, and longing sizzled through her.

This was more tangible than the shivery tingles she'd felt earlier; now it was a full-on craving and she couldn't stop herself from slightly leaning into him. The movement was small, so barely perceptible he might not have even noticed. But then his eyes arrested hers in the mirror, his pupils dilated, his gaze intensified. *He noticed.*

His voice was a soft growl in her ear. "What do you see in the mirror, Phoebe?"

An incredibly hot man more than capable of giving her a sexual adventure.

That's probably not what he means.

With their bodies so close, could he feel the quiver that went through her? She was turned on, and the longer they stood together, the more the ache of arousal intensified. She was tempted to shut her eyes, as if that would provide some escape, yet she couldn't look away from the picture they presented. He was broad shouldered and tall, but not enough to loom over her—a good height for kissing without craning her neck or having to stand on her toes. His naturally tan skin was a strong contrast to her pale complexion; their bodies tangled together would be like caramel-swirled cheesecake. Not that she planned to say any of that out loud.

She gave herself a mental shake, trying to regain her composure. Heath was giving her his time and effort to help her develop sensual confidence, and whether she thought this was the way to go about it or not, she owed him her cooperation. She obediently studied her reflection. "I see an attractive—"

"Beautiful."

Her lips twitched. "I thought this was about what *I* see."

"Well, since your vision is obviously fuzzy, I'm helping. Like glasses or contact lenses. Try again."

"I see a beautiful redhead with light brown eyes—"

"Your eyes are like antique gold, treasure capable of making men lose their minds."

"Oh, for pity's sake," she muttered, but it was difficult not to smile at his extravagant words. Was there any truth to them, or was all of the embellishment strictly to elevate her self-image? She looked hard at the mirror, attempting to view herself the way he described, to block out the chipped nail polish on her toes and the five extra pounds she didn't need and the way her bun had been knocked crooked from resting her head on the couch.

She reached for the rubber band that held her hair back. "I should have worn my hair down."

He caught her fingers. "I would normally agree with you—you have great hair—but you have a graceful neck, too." As he spoke, he trailed his knuckles across the curve of her neck. "Gives a man ideas. About doing this."

Transfixed, she watched him lower his dark head toward her, anticipation coiling tighter until his teeth grazed an excruciatingly sensitive spot below her jaw. Her legs buckled, and his hands came to her hips, holding her steady. The woman in the mirror was flushed, her lips parted, her hardened nipples visible through the silk of the tank top. The skirt she'd judged as practically conservative earlier in the evening now seemed like a tantalizing length. She couldn't help imagining Heath dropping his hands to the hem, inching the fabric upward so that his fingers could skate over the delicate flesh of her inner thighs. She trembled. He turned his head, his gaze momentarily meeting hers in their reflection, then he trailed open-mouthed kisses down the slope of her neck, stirring pleasure inside her that was almost dizzying in its intensity.

Her eyes slid shut, her total focus on the dual sensations of his mouth hot on her skin and the rock-hard erection pressed against her. She shifted her hips, unable to resist rubbing against him. His grip on her tightened, and he sucked in a breath before nipping at her collarbone. She might not be an experienced seductress, or the type of woman who had leather in her lingerie drawer, but she'd sure as hell aroused Heath.

You and how many other women?

The unwelcome thought chilled some of her ardor. "Wait." Her eyes opened, and she swayed forward, not quite moving out of his embrace, but no longer subtly rocking against him. It wasn't that she disapproved of Heath's affairs; his love life was between him and the women who'd eagerly shared it. She just wasn't sure she was ready to become one of their number.

His hands fell to his sides, and he rested his forehead lightly on her shoulder, not meeting her gaze in the mirror. She was grateful. She felt too raw to face him just yet.

But she couldn't stop herself from asking, "Wh-why did you do that?" Even though she'd asked for his help, she didn't want those kisses to be an act of charity. "I know we're pretending to date, but there's no audience here."

"The more accustomed you are to me touching you, the more comfortable you'll be when there *is* an audience. That's not the main reason I kissed you, though."

"No?"

"I wanted to," he said simply. "Selfish hedonist, remember? You felt damn good in my arms. But I'm not so selfish that I don't realize it's been a long day for you." He stepped away. "First a shift at work, then coming over here. I should let you get home to bed."

Just hearing him say *bed* caused her to feel achy and overheated. She nodded hastily. "Yeah, I should probably go." Tonight had given her a lot to think about.

"But I'll see you Thursday?" he asked. "For lunch?"

She'd almost forgotten about his awards luncheon. Technically, she worked Thursday, but she could go in a couple of hours late. The afternoon crowd was sparse. "Of course. I can meet you there."

"Wonderful." He moved to the side, watching as she slid her feet back in her discarded sandals.

"Lots of people from local restaurants will be there," he added, sounding annoyingly composed. Her senses were still rioting. "Cam will hear all about how I couldn't keep my eyes off you. You have my word, I'll be very convincing."

Of that, she had no doubt. For a brief, scorching moment, he'd nearly convinced her that she was the sexiest woman he'd ever held in his arms. Phoebe was beginning to think fooling others wouldn't be the difficult part. No, the trick would be not letting *herself* succumb to the illusion.

5

UNDER HEATH'S INFLUENCE, Phoebe was developing a dirty mind. Was it normal for a woman to be turned on while reading a description of the salad course—arugula with goat cheese, candied pecans and honey-drizzled peaches? It was just that, sitting next to Heath, with his arm balanced on her chair and his thumb idly sweeping over the nape of her neck, she was starting to get ideas about drizzling honey over his skin and licking it off. Or sucking it off his sticky-sweet fingers.

Trying to ignore the mild pulse of arousal between her legs, she shifted in her seat and reached for her goblet of ice water. Luncheon seating inside the refurbished 1920s mill had only begun a few moments ago, and most of the chairs at their table were still empty. Heath was discussing restaurant parking issues with a man who sat across from them, and Phoebe hoped she looked politely interested and not like someone mentally undressing her lunch companion. For the awards presentation, Heath was wearing a suit and tie, the expensive material perfectly tailored to show off the muscled body beneath it. He looked powerful. Sexy. She gulped more ice water.

She'd been uncertain what to wear—it was one thing to declare your intention to become a bold seductress, but that proclamation didn't come with a brand-new wardrobe. Besides, this was a professional daytime event; she would have looked ridiculous in a halter top and microskirt. The violet-blue sheath dress she'd chosen might not be the most daring fashion choice, but it was a flattering color. And she was pleased with her hairstyle. She'd started to leave her hair loose but, recalling the bone-melting pleasure of Heath's kisses the other night, she'd secured a heavy cascade of curls with a jeweled clip that left one side of her face bare and the slope of her neck exposed. She'd taken care with her makeup, too. Heath's description of her eyes—treasured antique gold—seemed to warrant more than a cursory brush of the mascara wand.

"Are these seats being saved for anyone?" a woman asked.

Phoebe turned to see an attractive brunette in her forties. A shock of white hair framed the right side of her face, giving her a distinctive appearance. "No. Please, join us."

"Gloria!" Heath stood so that he could come around the table and give the woman a hug. "Long time, no see, love. And is this your husband, Adam? Heard so much about you, sir." The two men shook hands, then Heath drew Phoebe forward, his arm lightly around her waist. "This is Phoebe Mars, my favorite pastry chef. If you've ever ordered dessert at Piri, it was probably one of Phoebe's masterpieces. Unfortunately, to try her dishes now, you'll have to find out who her new employer is. I could tell you, but I won't." He grinned mischievously. "I refuse to send customers to the competition."

"I'm at All the Right Notes," Phoebe interjected. "I have business cards in my purse. If you stop in this summer, dessert's on me."

Heath pressed a hand to his heart. "Why are the beautiful women always the most cruel?"

Gloria chuckled as they took their seats. "I can see you're good for him, dear. How did the two of you get together? Workplace romance?"

"Actually," Heath said, "Phoebe and I didn't fall for each other until after she defected from Piri. We ran into each other at a party, and she confessed her longstanding attraction."

"I what?" Phoebe turned sharply. It had been a strategic error to feign being a couple without first agreeing on a cover story. Heath was having entirely too much fun playing to their audience.

"Yes." He nodded solemnly. "She brought me a drink from the bar—"

"*You* brought me the drink."

"—and she said, 'I need you desperately.'"

By now, Phoebe was laughing outright, as were Gloria and her husband.

"'I want you, I crave you,'" he concluded with a

dramatic flourish. Then he beamed at Phoebe. "Isn't that how you remember it?"

"So close." She rolled her eyes. "You forgot the part where I threw myself at your feet."

"Forgot? Never." He gestured at the seats around them, including two that had been taken by newcomers while he spoke. "I just didn't want our friends here to think you came on too strong."

"Such a gentleman," she said wryly.

The next half hour followed in the same vein, with Heath holding court and keeping them all entertained. Yet Phoebe noticed that, while he led the conversation, he didn't keep the focus on himself. He asked Gloria if she was still considering expanding her restaurant franchise, and he recognized a young barista who'd just won a local award. When he congratulated her, the shy brunette blushed and mumbled that it was no big deal.

"Not true," Heath chided. "I had one of your artisanal coffees at the beverage trade show in March. Any awards you win are well deserved."

Her blush intensified, but her smile grew as he encouraged everyone to visit the independent coffee house where she worked.

He was even well versed in the building where today's awards were being held. While the shrimp-and-grits entree was being served, he told them stories about the company that had first built the mill to be close to the Atlantic Coast Line Railroad. Phoebe had never been here before and thought the venue was uniquely elegant despite the exposed brick, pine beams and concrete floor. Sunshine streamed through the skylights overhead, picking out threads of dark chocolate in Heath's hair, which looked black in dimmer light.

Like his hair color, Heath was more multifaceted than he appeared at first glimpse. He claimed to be cocky and selfish—and could be both on occasion—but those weren't his defining traits. If he was that one-dimensional, it would be a lot easier to remember that she wasn't really supposed to fall for him.

It's not really falling. It's just transferred affection. She'd been part of a couple for a long time. Heath's amusing company—and damn good looks—were an effective distraction, but could she possibly have recovered from her feelings for Cameron so quickly? *Wonderful. So you're in love with a chef who doesn't want you and lusting after a friend who's gallantly pretending to lust after you for the sake of your pride?*

Then again, there hadn't been anything pretend about the erection pressed against her at his loft. He'd wanted her. And it hadn't been just the impressive hard-on that proved it. Every stroke of his fingers on her skin and brush of his lips had made her feel desirable and powerfully feminine.

That antsy, achy feeling returned. At this rate, his joking story about how they'd started dating would become truth—she *would* need him desperately. Want him. Crave him. After how charming he'd been today, and how many times her thoughts had drifted this week to standing in front of that mirror with him, it was becoming impossible to remember why a fling with him would be more trouble than it was worth.

She pushed her chair back. "If you'll excuse me, I want to run to the ladies' room before the presentation starts." Her hormones could use the break from such close proximity to Heath.

When she walked into the restroom, a very tall woman glanced up from washing her hands. "Didn't I see you with Heath Jensen?" At Phoebe's nod, she sighed, "Lucky girl. I'm Starla Brown, sommelier for Gideon's Westside."

A stall door opened and an auburn-haired woman emerged, her sharp gaze zeroing in on Phoebe. "So you're Heath's latest?"

The tall woman frowned. "Don't be bitchy, Lianne. It's not her fault he never called you back." Her tone was gentle as she told Phoebe, "I hope this doesn't come as an unpleasant surprise, but Heath's sensual prowess is equaled only by his short attention span."

"Good Lord. Have you both slept with him?" The question escaped before Phoebe could censor herself. She'd known Heath dated a lot, but statistically, shouldn't she be able to walk into a public restroom without everyone there being a past lover?

Starla chuckled. "Neither of us, actually."

"Which is *none* of her business," Lianne grumbled.

"I monopolized his company at a thoroughly enjoyable restaurant opening last fall," Starla said, "but he wasn't interested enough to pursue anything. Lianne here made it through two dates, but…" She shrugged philosophically.

Lianne turned her frosty gray eyes back to Phoebe. "You might think you're going to be different, but trust me, honey, plenty of women thought that. He won't stick around."

Phoebe had grown up with an incredibly bitter woman lashing out at her; she wasn't about to take it from a stranger. "He might, he might not." She smiled broadly, channeling the confident, sexy woman she'd seen reflected in Heath's apartment. "In the meantime, the orgasms are phenomenal."

BIRDS WERE SINGING, and the sunshine was bright but not punishing as Heath climbed out of his car Friday morning. While climbing the stairs to Phoebe's apartment, he caught himself whistling a catchy pop hit and faltered on a cement step. *Damn, man, get it together.* What was next? Cartoon heart eyes?

At least he wasn't carrying flowers. Those would definitely be a sign that the line had blurred between their fake affair and real emotions. He enjoyed the hell out of Phoebe's company, but she was at least half in love with Cam still. Heath strongly disliked competition for his affections—call him a sore loser over his girlfriend jilting him for his stepbrother. Their wedding had been pure hell.

The reception might have been fun. He didn't remember much past the open bar.

So, no. He would not be bringing Phoebe roses. *Just plane tickets for a romantic getaway.* Yeah, much less confusing than flowers.

He knocked on the door, hoping he wasn't waking

her. Neither of them were morning people, but he had a meeting clear on the other side of the city at ten.

"Just a minute." Thankfully, the voice that called though the door was Phoebe's and not that of her brash roommate—the opinionated, baseball-loathing she-beast who'd taken one look at the way *he* looked at Phoebe and had given him the stink eye ever since. Clearly she had never trusted his intentions.

Insightful she-beast.

There was a pause while Phoebe presumably checked the security peephole, then the metallic slide of the chain and dead bolt. "Heath!" She smiled in greeting, but her gaze was quizzical. They were almost seeing as much of each other this week as when they'd worked together.

"Should I have called first?" The question was for form's sake. He hadn't phoned first because his persuasive skills were much stronger face-to-face.

"You know you're always welcome." She ushered him inside, and he enjoyed the sight of her legs in the short denim cut-offs she wore with an oversize Braves jersey. Her hair was wild, an untamed profusion of curls.

Following his gaze, she tugged on a ringlet and scowled. "I started to put on the ball cap that matches the jersey, but with the humidity today, I figured my hair would just launch the hat into the air like it was spring-loaded." She huffed in exasperation. "When I was a teenager, I had a little bit of bounce to my hair, but it's gotten crazier in the past few years. It's like, the more ruthlessly I pull it back for work, the more it rebels."

He nodded, siding with her hair. "Repression is bad for the soul."

She snorted. "Like *you* have any experience repressing your impulses?"

"More than you might think." For instance, he hadn't kissed her hello. That was a notable display of self-denial. He'd stolen a brief goodbye kiss yesterday, in full view of the luncheon guests, but he'd wanted to kiss her more thoroughly, to continue the sensual exploration they'd started in his loft. If she hadn't pulled away that night, how far would their encounter have gone?

"So what brings you by?" she said, walking into her kitchen. A coffee cup with steam still rising from it sat on her counter. She opened a cabinet and pulled out an empty mug, wiggling it by the handle in unspoken question.

He nodded, glancing around the modest apartment. "Is Gwen gone?"

"Yeah, left shortly after dawn. They need her on set for a twelve-hour shoot today. It's safe to speak freely," she teased.

"I'm here to ask you about a business trip—well, combination business and pleasure." His gaze slid back to her legs as he appreciated the toned muscle of her calves and her smooth thighs. "Cam and I are going to Miami a week from tomorrow. We'll be there a few days evaluating a couple of potential restaurant locations before flying back Wednesday. Come with me."

"Are you kidding?" She slammed the mug down hard enough that he winced, making a mental note to check his coffee for ceramic chips. "You, me and Cam? I was resistant to spending a few minutes with him at a party. And you're asking me to spend several days with the guy?"

"Let's evaluate your objectives," he coaxed. He tapped his index finger, counting off his first point. "You want to spend time with me and master the art of sexual confidence. We can do that in Miami, a hot, sensual city full of vibrant experiences. Two, you want to make Cam jealous. What's going to make him crazier than you and I canoodling on a beach with you in a revealing bikini?"

"I don't own a bikini."

"Easily solved." He tapped a third finger. "Finally, you've said that you don't know for sure if you even *want* him back. This could be the perfect time to decide once and for all. Maybe you'll surprise yourself and come home free of him." One could only hope. "In the meantime, I get your opinion on location, staffing, decorating… You know I think you're a great chef, Mars, but you have valuable input on lots of subjects, not just recipes."

She tried to hide a smile. "You are very difficult to turn down."

"That's just what your boss said."

"You talked to James already?"

"Well. It seemed pointless to invite you if you

couldn't get the time off work." He'd had to do some significant pleading, promising James that this was not a stealth attempt to rehire Phoebe. He'd also agreed to periodically mention to Piri diners who came in on weekends that All the Right Notes would be a great place to enjoy dessert and live music afterward. Plus, there'd been the outright bribe of a hundred-dollar bottle of pinot noir. "The trip wouldn't even affect Tuesday and Wednesday, since they're your days off, and we're leaving late enough Saturday that you could go in for dessert prep in the—"

"Stop! I don't need you to go behind my back or plan out my schedule." She tossed her hands in the air. "You totally pulled a Gwen. How did you two *not* hit it off? You're equally manipulative and diabolical and autocratic... As I hear these things out loud, I'm starting to realize I have terrible taste in friends."

"So we're flawed." He gave her a winning smile. "But we keep life interesting."

She stirred one and a half spoonfuls of sugar into his coffee, then passed the mug over to him. "The timing would be tight. I'm swamped with June weddings, although I guess if the flight was later in the day, I'd theoretically have time to deliver the two cakes I have scheduled. But even if I wanted to go, and that's a big if, the airfare—"

"Is taken care of." When her eyes widened, he made an impatient gesture. "I got a good deal. Seriously, my mother owns handbags that cost more than the round-trip ticket." After his father had died on a business trip, Rebecca Jensen hadn't hesitated to start spending life-insurance money. She'd wanted a second husband—a wealthy second husband—and she'd felt she should look the part. She'd told Heath that projecting success was a self-fulfilling prophecy, and he'd kept that in mind when he opened Piri. His mom was Rebecca Crawley now, married to an affluent software developer in Cary, North Carolina.

"And the flight isn't until three," he added. "The ticket is well worth it if it allows me to use you as a human shield. Cam is gifted in the kitchen, but I don't want to spend four days with only him for company. What if he asks about 'us'? And you know the first time we pass a street-food vendor, I'll have to listen to him rhapsodize about his fantasy of leaving the 'complicated restaurant world' and taking off in a food truck."

"Not that again. Doesn't he know how unsuited he'd be to something less superficially glamorous? The man loves having a big staff—"

Heath coughed and muttered, "Overcompensating" into his hand. It was more than the size of his staff that gave a man control.

She shot him a "what are you, twelve?" glare. "And he wants diners to savor his food, linger over it and pay him compliments at the end of the meal. He'd hate the hectic pace of a food truck."

"You're so intuitive. Which is why I need your input on the new restaurant possibilities. Oh, and did I mention the Braves will be in town playing the Marlins? I have two tickets. When was the last time you got out to a game?"

"You don't play fair, do you?"

"Hell, no." He winked at her over his coffee cup. "I play to win. Come with me to Miami. Please."

She glanced around the apartment, lips pursed as she considered the invitation. He tried not to stare at her mouth, remembering the kiss they'd shared at Bobbi's party, when he'd caught her off guard and she'd enthusiastically kissed him back. He wanted more of that heat and enthusiasm.

When she sighed and said, "I could use a vacation," he wanted to pump his fist in triumph.

"Maybe you should think of it as a vacation from real life," he coaxed. "An opportunity to explore."

Her eyes widened at his tone. "Why do I get the feeling you're not talking about South Beach sightseeing?"

"Because you know me well. You asked me to teach you to be sexy," he reminded her softly. "How hands-on do you want those lessons to be?"

"I…" When her gaze dropped to his hands, it took every ounce of his willpower not to reach for her. But if he came on too strong, she might change her mind about the entire trip. "The way you kissed me, the way you made me feel at your apartment—it was all wonderful, addictive even, but you're one of my closest friends. If we take this too far…"

"You're worried it will get complicated. It could, unless we both agree on clear parameters from the start."

She shifted her weight, looking equal parts intrigued and wary. "You mean like, what happens in Miami stays in Miami?"

"To borrow a cliché, yeah. There's a lot I could show you in four nights, Phoebe." He gripped the mug in his hand, momentarily overcome by all the ways he wanted to touch her. Pleasure her.

Color rising in her cheeks, voice breathy, she promised, "I'll think about it."

That makes two of us. He doubted he'd be able to think about anything else between now and when their plane landed next week.

"WELCOME TO VIVIEN'S ARMOIRE." A blonde in vertically striped jeans and a horizontally striped blouse stepped forward. "I'm Wren. Can I help you find anything today?"

Phoebe didn't get a chance to answer. Next to her, Gwen grumbled, "Yeah—point us toward the chastity belts."

Wren blinked. "Um…"

"I'll be browsing lingerie," Phoebe said, "but I also wanted to look at your swimsuits. I need a bikini."

"You need a suit of armor and a Taser."

"Gwendolyn! When I agreed to let you come with me, you promised to be helpful and keep your opinions about Heath to yourself."

"Sorry," her friend said unconvincingly. "I just worry that you're getting in over your head. A lot could happen on this trip."

Gwen's warning conjured Heath's words. *There's a lot I could show you, Phoebe.* She shivered. The more she thought about his offer, the more sense it made. Undoubtedly she was rationalizing, but who could blame her when a man that hot wanted to expand her sensual horizons?

"You don't have to worry about me," she told Gwen. "I'm an adult." She had no misconceptions about who Heath was. Frankly, the four nights they spent in Miami might qualify as one of his longer relationships.

Wren leaned toward Phoebe, her voice a stage whisper. "I empathize. I have two bossy older sisters."

"Hey," Gwen objected, "I'm not older. We're the same age!"

Phoebe smirked. "Guess I just seem like the younger, more carefree one."

Gwen pinched the bridge of her nose. "Wren, be my new best friend and tell me you have some booze hidden behind the counter?"

The other woman laughed. "No. But if you pull a flask out of your purse while you shop, I'll pretend not to notice. Best I can do." To Phoebe, she said, "Swimsuits are in the back left of the store, pajamas in the back right. Lingerie, as you can see, takes up the entire front half—if you need any fitting help, just call for me or Meg, my boss. And in case you're interested, our...specialty items are in the side room." She pointed to a closed door.

Phoebe's eyes widened at her impish tone. "I take it *specialty* isn't your fancy code for clearance racks."

"Hardly. Our specialty items make fun bachelorette party gifts. Or lively additions to romantic weekends away." She lowered her voice to a more confidential tone. "I have a brochure, if you'd like to look through it."

Gwen gripped Phoebe's shoulders and began propelling her forward. "Don't even think about it."

"Relax," Phoebe whispered to her roommate. "I didn't come here to buy sex toys."

Although, now that the topic had arisen, she couldn't help wondering about Heath's opinion on toys. Cam had known she owned a vibrator—she'd shyly mentioned it over drinks after they'd been together for months. His somewhat disdainful response had been, "What do you need that for, babe, when you've got me?" She'd never broached the subject of bringing it into bed with them.

Somehow, she suspected Heath would be more open-minded.

She grinned inwardly at the memory of him telling her he was unshockable. Gwen thought he was a bad influence—which was true—but he was also a wildly liberating influence. Promising not to judge, he'd encouraged her to be shameless in her pursuit of pleasure.

In the past, most of the sensory pleasure in her life had come from food. But in Miami, that was going to change.

6

"LAST CHANCE FOR an intervention where I talk some sense into you," Gwen said as her car rolled to a stop in the passenger drop-off lane outside Hartsfield-Jackson Airport.

Phoebe chuckled, enjoying the role reversal where she ran off with a man of questionable morals while Gwen was the one overthinking the situation. After the double shift Phoebe had pulled yesterday because she felt guilty for leaving James and the hours she'd spent this morning assembling multitiered wedding cakes at their respective reception venues, she should be exhausted. Instead, she couldn't remember the last time she'd felt so exhilarated. "Just tell me to have a good time."

"It better be a protected good time! Do you have condoms?"

"Heath and I have kissed." And would be doing that again soon. Anticipation rippled through her. "It's not a foregone conclusion that we'll be having sex. Necessarily."

Gwen arched an eyebrow.

"Okay, yes. I packed condoms." Many more than any two normal human beings could need for a four-day trip. *Just in case.* She blew Gwen a kiss. "Heath will drive me home when we get back Wednesday. If you're not working late, I'll fix us something yummy for dinner."

Inside the airport, she spotted him immediately. They'd agreed to meet by the ticket counter. He looked ready for the beach in white slacks and a boldly printed rayon shirt that was unbuttoned at the top; he hadn't shaved that morning, and the slight shadow made his already strong jaw look even more ruggedly masculine. It was difficult to pick a favorite between restaurateur Heath in his urbane suits and this Heath, who looked ready to buy a lady a drink at a tiki bar and have his way with her behind a sand dune.

Although she'd worn a simple jewel-toned tunic over capris for the flight, she looked forward to showing off some of her own beach attire in Miami— including the brand-new push-up bikini that had made even Gwen say, "Damn, girl, spectacular boobs."

Boarding passes in hand, they headed for the security line. "Want me to get your suitcase for you?" Heath asked, nodding toward the roller bag she planned to stick in an overhead compartment.

She gave him a perplexed look. "Why?" It wasn't as if she was carrying something heavy—and, even if she had been, her arms were toned from habitually lugging five-pound bags of sugar and industrial-size sacks of flour. "It has wheels."

"Exactly." His eyes twinkled. "Making it easy to pull. With almost zero effort on my part, I still get to look chivalrous. Win-win."

After passing through the checkpoint and body scan, they retrieved their belongings from the conveyor belt and took an escalator down to the trams that carried passengers to their terminal. Looped straps hung from the ceiling, and a mechanical voice advised them to "hold on."

Heath shot her a grin, his gaze traveling down her body in an almost palpable caress. "The recording just said hold on, it didn't specify what I'm supposed to hold on *to*." Leaning against a metal pole, he dropped his hands to her waist and pulled her close, his fingers grazing her butt.

A sense of gratification filled her, as if she'd been waiting for this moment—for his touch—ever since she woke up. She cupped the back of his head and tugged him toward her, sucking lightly at his bottom lip before sliding her tongue into his mouth, twining it with his. Heath groaned softly, his grip on her ass tightening.

"I want that vacation from reality," she whispered. Four nights to explore each other, to discover her sexier side and indulge in pleasure. "But do we have to wait until we get to Miami to start it?"

In answer, he kissed her again. It was intense, but brief, in deference to the handful of passengers at the other end of the train and the fact that their tram was stopping.

"This is us," Heath said, his eyes gleaming hungrily as he stared down at her. "Unless you want to do another loop around the airport and make out some more?"

Yes, please. "We should get off." Her cheeks burned. "Of the tram, I mean."

His laugh was a husky promise. "Tram exit now. Later for the other."

As they walked to their gate, he shifted his tote bag so that he could hold her hand. The simple, innocent gesture left her grinning like an idiot. *Wait— you're too happy.* The nagging inner voice sounded a lot like Gwen.

Happy is good, Phoebe told herself.

Happy is an emotion, a risk. You're supposed to keep it physical. A rebound fling. Sexual tutoring. No developing feelings! She couldn't just unpack emotions after the trip and shove them in a drawer alongside her bikini and new lingerie.

"Phoebe, Heath, you made it." Cam stood under the gate number sign in a polo shirt and starched khakis. His greeting turning to a glower when he noticed their joined hands.

She'd seen the two men together so many times, but now she felt as if she was viewing them with new eyes. Cam's hair was, as usual, gelled to perfection, and it looked as if he'd done some spray tanning since Bobbi's party. He was a very handsome man, but where Heath was sexy in a raw, natural way, with his defined jaw and bold features, Cam's attraction seemed calculated. In an up-close comparison, he looked as if he was trying too hard.

Heath raised Phoebe's hand to his lips and pressed a quick kiss to her knuckles. "I'm going to grab a bottle of water for the flight. Want one?"

"Yes, thanks."

He turned to his business partner. "Cam?"

The other man flashed a tight smile. "No, I think I'll wait and get something stronger on the plane."

As Heath jogged toward the nearest gift shop, heavy awkwardness descended. She searched her mind for something to say. "How's Dana?"

Cam blinked. "Who?"

"Your date to the party?" *The woman you invited to one of my closest friend's birthdays less than two weeks after dumping me?*

"I haven't spoken to her since Bobbi's." His tone was rueful. "I'm afraid I didn't make a very good impression on her, since I spent most of that evening staring at you. You looked incredible."

She made a note to tell Gwen her makeover efforts had been a success. Cam might not be "crawling back," but he looked like a man with regrets. Was it cruel what she was doing, coming along on this trip as Heath's date? *If Cam hadn't ditched you, you could be here now as* his *date.* Try as she might, she couldn't imagine having kissed him so enthusiastically on the tram.

"So." He cleared his throat. "You and Heath. I didn't see that development coming."

She thought about the moment Heath's mouth had met hers at the birthday party. "No one was more shocked than me."

"Are the two of you...serious?"

Serious. Hardly a word that was applicable to a fake relationship with a serial-dating commitment-phobe. "We're having fun. I need some of that in my life right now." There was an edge of anger in her voice, and she didn't try to temper it. While he'd never been obligated to stay in a relationship that made him unhappy, there were less duplicitous ways he could have ended things. Was he even sorry? "You hurt me. And you cost me a job I loved."

"But I heard that things are going well for you over at Notes."

"What if they weren't? Why weren't you just honest with me, Cameron? I'm a professional. You didn't have to give me a song and dance about us having a future together."

"Maybe I was just worried that future was coming at us too fast. Maybe I panicked."

There was a vulnerable note she wasn't used to hearing in his tone. For a second, she almost felt bad for him. Then she remembered that he'd spent a couple of weeks convincing her that their "long-term" relationship would be healthier if they didn't spend every waking hour together, sending her on a job search that might not have worked out as fortuitously as it had. Days on end of deliberately misleading her wasn't panic; it was self-serving premeditation.

"I won't blame you if you say no," he said, "but,

after this trip, can I call you sometime?" He gave her a smile that was sad and sweet and reminded her of why she'd fallen for him in the first place. Cam was not without his charms. But then he added, "I could cook for you! I have new dishes that need your feedback."

Any lingering sympathy she'd felt hardened. Two years together and her main role to him was still taste tester? "Call if you want, but I might be busy." *Busy moving on with my life.*

PHOEBE GLANCED OUT the small rectangular window, watching as the plane sped down the runway. "I still can't believe I let you buy me a plane ticket."

"It's not like I splurged on first class," Heath said.

"Feels pretty luxurious not having to share our row with anyone." Their side of the plane included only two seats, without a passenger crammed into the dreaded middle. If she thought too hard about it, she'd wonder how the other side of the aisle—with three people in every row—didn't unbalance the plane. She preferred not to dwell on that while they were taking off. "Plus, even if we're not in first class, the service has been excellent." Had that observation sounded acerbic?

Honestly, it was almost insulting how the flight attendant doted on him. Phoebe could certainly understand Heath's appeal, but wasn't it unseemly to flirt with a man who was traveling with a girlfriend? *Not that I am his girlfriend.* But the flight attended couldn't know that. He played the part of affectionate lover beautifully. At the gate, Cam had looked livid every time Heath casually touched her or smiled in her direction. She was relieved Cam's seat was in a different section of the plane, giving her a two-hour reprieve from his dour mood.

The plane sharply ascended, and she sucked in a breath.

"You okay?" Heath asked. "You should have warned me you were a nervous flyer."

"I'm not really any kind of flyer. I can count on one hand the number of times I've been on a plane." She and Gwen had grown up in south Georgia and come to Atlanta together after high school. Most places Phoebe had visited outside the state she'd reached by driving.

"Guess it makes sense that when I asked about the most adventurous thing you've done, the mile-high club wasn't on your list." He grinned. "Lack of opportunity."

"And extreme lack of interest. Having sex in a tiny lavatory that's been used by countless strangers is *not* a turn-on for me."

"Not as tempting as, say, a man watching—"

"Hey!" Her face heated. Could any of the surrounding passengers hear what they were discussing?

"I didn't bring it up to make you uncomfortable. I wanted to know about your other fantasies. Do you have a…like a bucket list of sexual activities you want to try someday? A 'fucket' list, so to speak."

She pressed her hand over her mouth to smother an unladylike burst of laughter. She wouldn't want the overly solicitous flight attendant to rush over and ask Heath if the noisy redhead was bothering him.

"There is something," Phoebe admitted. Maybe what she yearned for didn't qualify as a fantasy in the way Heath meant—this wasn't about a crazy location or a battery-operated sex toy—but she'd just had a revelation about her own desires.

Growing up, she'd been conditioned to be modest and demure. In college, she'd had hushed sex because the dorm walls were thin. And Cam was…almost too airbrushed for real life. He was a considerate lover, taking her orgasms as his responsibility, but he wasn't spontaneous or uninhibited. She understood wanting to brush his teeth before they kissed in the morning— could even applaud it—but was it really necessary to floss *and* gargle mouthwash for exactly three minutes before they could consider morning sex? To rationalize his fussiness, she'd told herself she was glad he cared about hygiene and personal maintenance. But it was impossible to get lost in sex when she was worried it would be gauche to sweat on her partner.

"Am I supposed to guess?" Heath traced the shell of her ear with the tip of his index finger, a feathery, barely there touch that made her tremble in her seat. "I'll start naming the naughtiest things I can come up with, and you tell me if I'm getting warmer."

There was a terrifying idea. "I want sex that's… not polite." When he raised an eyebrow, she elaborated, "I don't want to cringe if it gets a little loud or messy or rowdy."

In contrast to her wish for a noisy rumpus, her

voice was barely a whisper. Heath was leaned in close to catch every word.

"The heat of passion isn't the time to be politically correct," she said. "I don't want a guy who stops to give a formal apology because he accidentally pulled my hair." Frankly, there were a few instances where a little hair pulling might be a turn-on. "Gallantry is great in real life, and respect is essential. But in a hot moment, it would be empowering to know I drove a man to be dirty and out of control."

"Dirty like you have sex after a workout without showering first?" Heath asked against her ear. "Or dirty like your lover tells you he wants to go down on you and can't wait to discover how your pussy tastes?"

"Heath!" Flames swept through her body. The formerly well-behaved Phoebe might have mistaken it for mortification, but the pulse at her core was pure arousal.

"What?" he asked, his expression all innocence— the devil smiling beatifically while tucking her soul in his back pocket. "It was hypothetical."

"It was vulgar."

"You're grinning." He rubbed his thumb across her bottom lip, tracing her smile, and she melted at his touch, liquid need simmering inside her.

Oh, yeah. We're gonna need those condoms.

AS IT TURNED OUT, hours of sexual frustration—and watching the doe-eyed flight attendant do everything but write her phone number on Heath's pack of peanuts—left a person cranky. When they exited the plane, Phoebe's entire body felt too hot and too tight. The sticky Miami air as they waited for a cab did nothing to improve her mood. Neither did Cam's announcement that he'd texted Miranda, who couldn't wait to see them, "especially Heath."

"Who's Miranda?" Phoebe asked, pulling the silky fabric of her top away from her back in a futile attempt at ventilation.

"The leasing agent," Heath said with a frown at Cam. "We're meeting with her tomorrow. This evening, our plan is to check in, clean up and have dinner at the place Cam and I are leaning toward buying."

Cameron wasn't interested in the itinerary. He was telling Phoebe, "Miranda is smitten with Heath— even offered to let him bunk with her on his visits down here instead of staying at a hotel. That's probably not a service she offers all her clients. But the ladies love him, right?"

Phoebe thought of Lianne and Starla at the awards luncheon and ground her teeth.

"Now that I stop to think about it," Cam said, "Miranda's actually quite pretty."

"Maybe you should ask her out while we're here," Heath encouraged with a pointed smile. "Since you're single and alone."

Phoebe climbed into the taxi and prayed the ride was a quick one; otherwise all the testosterone in the vehicle might suffocate her before they ever reached their destination.

Her irritation faded a bit once they pulled up in

front of their coastal boutique hotel. It wasn't as tall as its high-rise neighbors, but the balconies on the ten-story building should afford a gorgeous view of the water. The art deco architecture and lobby were charmingly retro, and she looked forward to seeing her and Heath's room.

The woman behind the check-in counter took Heath's ID and company credit card. "We have you down for an ocean-view room with a king-size bed."

"King-size bed?" Phoebe squeaked, feeling immediately foolish over her involuntary reaction. She'd known they were sharing a room. What had she expected, that they'd share side-by-side beds like some couple in a '50s TV show? Still, until this exact moment, sleeping in the same bed as Heath had been more of an abstract idea. Or a hot fantasy.

"Is there a problem?" the hotel employee asked.

"Is there?" Cam echoed from his spot down the counter. Did he sound hopeful?

"No problem whatsoever," Heath told the woman, putting his arm around Phoebe's waist as he glanced in Cam's direction. "With this being a smaller hotel, we were afraid all the king-size rooms would be booked. She's excited."

Phoebe nodded wordlessly. She also refrained from comment when, after the woman outlined the bar and dining options on property and suggested her favorites, Heath responded with "Thanks, sweetheart." Still, despite keeping a tactful silence, Phoebe found her temper rising along with the elevator as she and Heath rode to the eighth floor.

By the time he unlocked their door, he was casting her wary looks. "Okay," he said as he closed the door behind them, "is it having one bed that's pissing you off, or am I missing something?"

"I don't recall saying I was pissed." She let her suitcase and tote bag fall to the side and marched past the bed toward the balcony doors. Even feeling prickly and agitated, she could appreciate the gorgeous view. The blues and greens of the water were soothing. The man behind her? Not so much.

He sat on the edge of the mattress. "Talk to me, Phoebe."

Just Phoebe.

She whirled around. "You do know it's patronizing to call women *sweetheart*, don't you?" All the females around him were "love" and "beautiful." *Except for me*. Good thing she and Heath weren't really a couple. It would be maddening to tolerate his constant, reflexive flirting.

He blinked. "Sorry. I'm not intentionally condescending, just Southern. I would have stopped if I'd realized they minded."

To be fair, the flight attendant had not minded a bit when she'd handed him his soda and he'd responded with "Thanks, darling." She had openly beamed. So why was Phoebe righteously indignant on her behalf? *Would you really have been so bothered if the flight attendant had been twenty or thirty years older?*

She studied the yellow geometric print on the carpet. "You…never call me any of those things."

"Wait." He stood, looking more agitated. "You're *complaining*? Because I don't 'patronize' you?"

"No, of course not. I'm not insane."

His expression was skeptical.

"It's just funny, don't you think? You do it as a force of habit, probably never even realizing half the time that you're saying those things. But I guess since I was dating Cam, you were subconsciously careful not to call me anything that could be construed as…"

He walked toward her, shaking his head. "I said plenty of flirty things when the two of you were together, and you know it. And you're right, I call lots of women 'sweetheart.' Or 'gorgeous.' It's meant to be friendly, like the female version of calling a guy 'dude' or 'bro,' I guess. You, Phoebe Mars…" He glanced away momentarily, but when he met her eyes again, the intensity in his gaze was searing. "You are beyond random endearments. You're special and one of a kind."

She swallowed, startled by the rising tide of emotion inside her. God, she wasn't going to embarrass herself by getting teary, was she? She hadn't expected him to say something so sweet. "I forget sometimes what a nice guy you are."

His laugh was strained. "I've had a hundred thoughts about you since you walked into the airport this afternoon. Not a single damn one of them was nice."

He cupped her face in his hands, holding her a willing captive as his mouth took hers in a deep, ravishing kiss that sent white-hot lust through her. She clung to him, almost painfully eager for more. While his tongue plundered her mouth, wringing a soft cry of encouragement from her, his hand dipped beneath the hem of her top, skating over her bare abdomen and upward until he reached the satin of her bra. He palmed her breast through the fabric, which felt good at first, but it wasn't enough, not nearly enough, and she felt feverish as she arched into his touch.

"Heath." The way she sighed his name was a plea.

As he kissed her, he walked them backward. He stopped at the foot of the bed, breaking contact long enough to lift her shirt over her head and let it flutter to the floor. His gaze locked on her breasts and the emerald-green demibra she'd bought this week, his avid expression justifying every dime she'd spent on the high-end lingerie.

He skimmed his thumb beneath a lace edge, lightly brushing her nipple, and she shuddered. She wouldn't care if he ripped off the expensive bra, shredding it in the process, if it meant nothing between his touch and her skin. She slid the straps down her arms, exposing more of her breasts. He rewarded her boldness by lowering his head and swirling his tongue around one agonizingly sensitive tip. *So good.* What had started as a sharp twinge of arousal between her legs was becoming a rush of wet heat.

Obviously she wasn't the only one who craved skin-to-skin contact. After unhooking her bra, he whipped off his own shirt and pulled her closer to kiss her again. Dark hair dusted his sculpted chest, and the light abrasion of it against her bare breasts made her want to rub herself against him like a cat seeking affection. She didn't doubt that an evening in Heath's arms would make her purr.

He pulled them down across the mattress but didn't cover her body with his own. Instead, he propped himself on his elbow, his face close to hers. "I don't want you to be upset about just having the one bed."

"Not upset at all." The overwhelming sensations he lavished on her didn't leave room for an iota of discontent.

"We may be sharing the bed," he said, his expression solemn, "but we don't need to have sex."

"What?" Could she have sounded more distraught? *Way to have some pride, Pheeb.* Screw pride. She wanted to get laid. "But don't you want—"

He slid her hand to the front of his pants, pressing it to the steely ridge of his cock. "I want." Closing his eyes, he bucked his hips, grinding his erection again her hand. The raw need etched on his face was so harshly beautiful it made her burn.

Then he opened his eyes, rolling atop her. "We're only in Miami a few days. I plan to touch you plenty— I plan to make you shake with desire and cry out my name—but we can stop shy of sex. Maybe it will be easier to resume our regularly scheduled friendship if we don't cross that line."

He kissed the column of her throat, nuzzling lower until he'd reached the curve of her breast. "I'm being noble." He caught her nipple between his thumb and finger, making her gasp. "Sort of."

"But—" She didn't get very far because his mouth

moved over her breast, claiming the hardened peak, and all rational thought dissolved.

Very soon she *was* shaking with desire. He alternated between one side and the other, feasting, as if he couldn't get enough of her. She writhed beneath him, so passion dazed that it took her a moment to register that he was trying to slide down her pants. She gave an obliging wiggle of her hips, desperate for his touch where she was wet and aching. He stroked her through the lace, the damp fabric a silky slide against her swollen clitoris.

Then he began kissing a path down her stomach, and anticipation stuttered through her as he inched the lacy bikini briefs over her thighs, easing them slowly down her calves and ankles as if he had all the time in the world. He slid her legs wider apart, making room for himself, and gave her a deliciously evil smile. Even though he didn't repeat his dirty words from the plane, she heard them in her head as if he was telling her now how eager he was to taste her.

But he didn't rush, licking across her upper thigh, then parting the slick folds to find the tight bundle of nerves. He lapped at her until she couldn't imagine any sweeter torture in the world, then scraped his teeth over her clit, making her whimper. Her body throbbed, unable to contain the pleasure he gave, and when he sucked hard, he might as well have pressed a detonation button. Her hips jolted off the bed, undulating against his mouth as she came in an explosive blast of sheer carnal bliss.

Instead of stopping, he slid two fingers inside her,

moving in time to the rhythmic spasms that rippled through her while continuing to stroke her with his tongue. If she could have caught her breath, she might have protested—*too much, too much*—but then she was somehow hurtling up the ascent again and spiraling over the edge with a shriek she tried to muffle against her hand.

Wow.

She blinked up at the ceiling, slowly regaining her senses, if not the use of her extremities. That second orgasm had melted her muscles into a puddle of contentment.

Heath rose from the bed, crossing to the minibar and returning with two cold bottles of water. He smiled down at her. "Thought you could use one of these."

She nodded. At least, she meant to. She wasn't sure her head moved. "You might have to open it for me." He did, and she took a grateful sip, then sighed happily. "I'm afraid I won't be able to help you evaluate that restaurant tonight. Going out to eat would require moving." Not happening. "Bring me back lots of pictures on your phone and a to-go entrée, would you?"

"How could I possibly leave this room if you're here naked in bed?" He set down his own water and took her hand, brushing a kiss over the pulse point in her wrist before pulling her into a sitting position. "Come on, you. You'll feel restored after a shower." He fingered the tangled curls that fell forward over her shoulder. "I'll even help you wash your hair."

She eyed him suspiciously. "*Only* my hair. After

orgasms that intense, I'm too tender for you to 'wash' anything else right now."

He gave her his patented look of innocence. "I promise. But for the record? You have permission to wash any part of me that you want."

Her gaze traveled down to the front of his pants. He was still visibly erect, and she felt a thrill of impatience over the chance to make him feel as good as he'd just made her feel. She shot to her feet. "What are we waiting for?"

7

SINCE PHOEBE HAD asked for a moment alone in the bathroom, Heath took off his remaining clothes in the middle of their suite, letting them fall to the carpet. He was trying to tamp down regrets about his choice not to keep Phoebe in bed and make love to her until she couldn't walk. He'd told her he was trying to be noble by not having sex.

It wasn't a complete lie.

Rounding the bases was one thing, but he didn't want her to go home feeling like they'd done something irrevocable that damaged their friendship. And given Cam's evident jealousy earlier, it was probable the man would try to win her back. If the two eventually reconciled, Heath didn't want her to feel, however irrationally, like she'd cheated.

And what about the other half of your reason? The part that wasn't noble at all, but pure self-preservation. At every family holiday, Heath had to watch a woman he'd once loved sit next to his brother,

her head on Victor's shoulder as she smiled up at him. Heath wasn't in love with Phoebe, but sex between them wouldn't be meaningless. She was a longtime friend, and he cared deeply about her. If he had to see her back in her ex's arms, he'd rather do it without being taunted by the memory of making love to her.

But that didn't prevent them from enjoying the hell out of each other.

He heard the shower start running, and then the bathroom door opened. Phoebe had wrapped one of the generous white hotel towels around herself. Her innate modesty made him chuckle since five minutes ago he'd been caressing and licking her naked body.

"I—" She drew up short, sucking in a breath at the sight of his own nakedness. *"Oh."* Her gaze roamed greedily over him, the desire in her eyes like a fever in his blood. She swung the door wider and grinned impishly. "Get in here."

He immediately complied. "Anyone ever tell you that you're sexy when you're bossy?" He threaded his hands through her hair, tilting her face upward for a kiss. When she realized that he'd surreptitiously loosened her towel and let it drop, she bit his bottom lip. He drew back with a smirk. "It's not like you were planning to shower in the towel, right?"

"Maybe I was planning to do a seductive striptease for you," she joked.

"End result accomplished. Although, if you'd like to do one when we get back tonight…"

Her hair was so long that the ends of it coyly covered her breasts. He trailed his hand through a ringlet, lightly grazing a nipple.

"Mmm." Phoebe closed her eyes. "I thought you promised to behave."

"Did I? That doesn't sound like me." He pushed her hair back over her shoulders for an unimpeded view of her, and the light caught the myriad shades, from auburn to a few pale strands of blond. "You have the most gorgeous hair." He had a sudden vivid fantasy of it wrapped around his fist while she took him in her mouth.

He reached for the handle of the shower door. "I'm getting in." He wasn't sure if the water was warm yet, but frankly, cold might do him some good.

The shower was tiled in expensive-looking marble and generously sized, easily big enough for two. He stepped inside and couldn't help thinking how good life was when the gorgeous redhead joined him. The spray of water was hot, but not nearly as hot as his desire for Phoebe.

She leaned into his chest, running her tongue over his collarbone. "I've always thought you were a good dresser. Now I think it's a shame you're legally required to wear clothes in public. Maybe I can write the governor, get some kind of exception made."

He laughed. Her personality was like her hair, so many different interwoven hues, from gentle shyness to bold passion to bright humor. His amusement took a backseat to arousal, though, when she raked her nails over his chest and the sensitive skin of his stom-

ach. Then she reached for the sandalwood-scented
bar of soap.

"So I get to wash you anywhere I want?" Her voice
was breathy, her whiskey-gold eyes focused on his
dick.

He nodded, fighting the urge to reach for her hand
and place it on him. *Patience.* He didn't want to rush
her. Of course, in the meantime, he was quietly losing
his mind and shaking with lust. But that didn't seem
to bother her. She took her sweet time lathering up a
palm full of suds, then dropped her hand...to skate
across his thighs, going out of her way to avoid the
erection almost pulsing for her touch.

He gritted his teeth. "Evil tease."

She smiled, looking delighted. "No one ever calls
me evil." As if in reward, she slid one finger along
his shaft. Then she encircled him with her hand, and
his head fell back against the cool marble of the wall,
his hips flexing of their own accord. All too soon, she
let go of him. "I can't reach your back if you stand
like that," she chided.

He growled low in his throat but obediently moved.
It was almost too much of a turn-on to see her take
charge to complain that she was no longer touching
him. *Almost.* She did wash his back, turning it into a
sensual massage that gradually reached his ass. She
stroked loving circles across his glutes before reaching between his legs to cup his balls, scraping a fin-
gernail over him. He hissed in his breath and whirled
around, backing her into the corner.

"Oh, dear." Her eyes widened with mock alarm. "I pushed you too far. Or not far enough?"

Her now-wet hair concealed much of her torso and when she grinned up at him with that mischief in her gaze, droplets of water decorating her skin in erotic constellations he wanted to trace with his lips, she looked like a debauched mermaid. *My mermaid.* Whomever Phoebe might decide to be with in the future, right at this moment, she belonged to him. He placed a hand on either side of her and leaned in to kiss her breathless.

It was an uncivilized kiss. His tongue thrust deep, and their teeth clicked together. Far from complaining, she reached down and gripped him, her thumb running over the head of his cock and making him moan into her mouth. Eyes closed, he rocked into her wet, slippery hand while she squeezed, moving her fist up and down the length of him. Her touch was like lightning, sizzling him to a crisp, but he'd stand here forever as long as she kept…doing…that.

His balls tightened, and his orgasm built and he surprised himself by giving in to a raw urge to push her hand away, turning her so that she faced the wall, pinned between the tile and his body. He nipped at her shoulder, his hands coming up to cup her breasts hard, and he rubbed himself against the lush curves of her ass. Then he came in a blinding rush across her silky skin, his bellow of satisfaction echoing in the marbled stall. Afterward, he rested his head atop hers and waited for the dark spots to clear from his vision.

Phoebe was breathing as hard as he was. "Well. That was—"

"Sticky?" He turned the showerhead to aim the hot water across her skin, washing her clean.

"I was going to say, erotic as hell." She smiled over her shoulder. "But your description's accurate, too."

IT WAS PROBABLY a blessing that Phoebe had ultimately decided to go curly tonight and not use her flatiron. The way she kept staring into space, replaying the past hour and a half with Heath, she'd probably burn off whole sections of her hair if she was trying to straighten it. *Get it together*, she ordered herself. She raised the tube of liquid liner toward her face and realized she was about to outline the same eye she'd already done.

Good grief. One would think she'd never had an orgasm before—or, to be completely accurate, three.

The two in bed had been followed by another when Heath had insisted on helping her dry off after the shower. Interestingly, his version of drying had left her very wet. The man had amazing fingers. Glancing at the knotted sash of her wrap dress, she could easily picture those fingers untying the sash after dinner. She should be too satisfied to feel aroused again, yet renewed anticipation coursed through her.

Did Heath feel this same insatiable need? With his wealth of experience, she could understand if he was less dramatically affected than she was. Then again, in the shower… She shivered at the memory. He'd been almost primal with her, and she wasn't used to inspiring that kind of passion. To have a man as sexy as Heath stare down at her with such intense hunger was downright intoxicating.

She'd locked herself away in the bathroom to get ready so that she could surprise him with the finished look. If anything in her wardrobe would make a man insatiable for her, it was this ruched dress that was all red on her left side and white with the faint outline of red flowers on her right. The neckline crisscrossed over a brand-new push-up bra in a way that made her cleavage look like a contender for the eighth wonder of the world. The hemline mimicked the same crisscross, folding over her thighs and creating a provocative slit when she walked. Feeling inspired by the colorful vibe of Miami, she'd worn more dramatic makeup than usual, finishing off the look with high-heeled sandals Gwen had grudgingly let her borrow and bangle bracelets that provided a soundtrack for her movements.

As she studied her reflection, her lips parted in a shimmery, bright red smile. "I think that's officially as good as it's going to get." She reached for the doorknob and emerged from the bathroom. "Ready!"

The remote control Heath had been using to flip through channels hit the ground with a thud. "Whoa." His gaze traveled the length of her body and back to meet her eyes, slowing to appreciate his favorite spots on the return trip. "How am I going to concentrate on this restaurant I'm supposed to be evaluating when you look like that?"

She smoothed her hand over the skirt and batted her eyelashes. "So I look all right?"

Giving her a smile of blindingly wicked intent, he crooked his index finger. "Come closer and ask me that, Phoebe."

"Oh, no." Giggling, she made a dash for the door. "We have reservations." Not to mention Cam waiting for them in the lobby. She'd practically forgotten about him. Heath had a way of holding a woman's entire focus.

They got into the elevator with three men in suits, and she could feel one of them casting her surreptitious glances, his admiration obvious although he didn't speak to her. The businessmen got off two floors before the lobby, and Heath laughed as soon as they were gone.

"Poor bastard," he said sympathetically. "Could he have been more obvious? Be careful how you wield your powers. This temptress makeover of yours is going to be rough on mere mortal men."

She smiled at the flattery, but at the same time, she couldn't help contrasting his reaction to how *she* would have felt if they'd been in the elevator with an ogling woman. During their flight, she'd been irritated by the flight attendant's clear attraction to Heath. Yet he wasn't the tiniest bit jealous. "You're not bothered that he liked what he saw?"

"I'm proud of you. This is what you wanted, to become more seductive. I believe your exact wording was 'va va voom.'" He gave her an assessing once-over. "Mission accomplished."

Right. His words were completely logical, in keeping with the objectives they'd agreed on. Why had she expected a different response? Just because she and Heath had shared a phenomenal afternoon didn't mean he wanted to keep her for himself. *That's what a fling is*, she reminded herself. Impermanent.

I'm not upset. She just wasn't experienced with this kind of affair and needed a moment to adjust her expectations. When the elevator reached the lobby, she hurriedly exited, trying to stay in front of Heath until she could marshal her expression into a more believable smile. Cam was waiting outside the elevator bank and his eyes widened as soon as he saw her.

"Phoebe! You look incredible." He took both her hands in his, his expression approving. "Miami's known to have some very exclusive clubs—places you can't get into without being on the VIP list—but I swear there's nowhere in the city that wouldn't let you past the velvet ropes tonight."

"Thank you." She found herself oddly glad that Cam was with them for the cab ride to the restaurant. She'd overreacted in the elevator, letting herself be disappointed by Heath's pragmatic attitude, but that was just because she'd been so caught up in the passion of their afternoon together. Exchanging small talk with Cam gave her time to regain perspective.

It was funny to think that, just two weeks ago, she'd been anxiety-ridden about having to face her ex at Bobbi's party. He'd meant something different to her then. Now that more time had passed, she was able to enjoy friendly conversation with him, sharing the things they had in common without the emotional weight of worrying about their relationship.

When the cab pulled up to the restaurant, there were already waiting diners clustered outside with glowing pagers to let them know when their tables were ready. A crowd was a good sign. Heath had told her there were two possible restaurants in the area that he and Cam might buy and rebrand. This was the first, a place that had been run by the same family for over twenty years. The owner wanted to retire, and neither of his grown children had interest in taking it over. Before Heath invested in it, he needed to check out what kind of crowd it drew, the neighborhood it was in, the parking available—all logistics that could make or break a restaurant. The other potential place they were considering was a restaurant that had gone under, which had the advantage of a much lower price point.

"But then there's the curse to consider," Heath had told her on the plane today.

If a restaurant made a bad first impression on patrons, it was difficult to overcome negative perceptions even with new management, complete refurbishment and a different menu. "I'm tempted to take it on just because I like a challenge," he'd said, "but then I remembered that I like profits more."

Because Heath and Cam were in talks with the owners to take over this restaurant, Phoebe had no doubt that they could have made a special reservation and had a table waiting for them even on a packed Saturday night. But she wasn't surprised when they gave her name to the hostess at the podium and didn't mention who they were. Anonymity provided a chance to more accurately evaluate the service, offering Heath and Cam an idea of which members of the waitstaff they wanted to keep on and which might be put on notice. Phoebe knew firsthand that Heath was a loyal employer who helped keep the people working for him energized, but he expected hard work in return. He was cheerfully demanding.

In bed, too, she thought with a grin. Even after she'd thought she was sated this afternoon, he'd pushed her further than she'd realized she could go. What would actual sex be like with that much intensity? She found herself staring at him while he talked to Cam about seating capacity and table configurations. When Heath's gaze caught hers, he did a double take and she knew that part of what she was thinking must be visible on her face. Heat spread through her, but she didn't glance away. Instead, she just smiled, eyes still locked with his. His comment about high-top tables not providing an intimate enough setting faltered, and he took a half step toward her.

Cam frowned. "Everything okay?"

"It's warm in here," Heath said. "I think I'll grab us some drinks at the bar. Want a beer?"

"Drinks sound good," Cam said. "But I think I want to try their jalapeño mojito."

Nodding, Heath turned to Phoebe. But when she opened her mouth to ask for a glass of wine, he took her hand. "You can help me carry them," he said tersely. Then he led her away. As soon as they'd

rounded the corner into the small, dim hallway sep-
arating the bar from the main dining room, he captured her face in his hands, his mouth descending
on hers, ravenous. Their tongues tangled together,
and desire quickened in her abdomen, melting lower.

He released her almost as quickly as he'd grabbed
her, but even that brief kiss had been enough to leave
her quivering for more.

"Sorry." He actually looked startled, which was
rare for him. "Lost my head for a second."

Because of me. She grinned up at him, wanting
him even more than before. He'd told her this afternoon that they shouldn't have sex while they were in
Miami—but he'd also assured her that mere mortal
men wouldn't be able to resist her. Phoebe wouldn't
call Heath "mere" anything, but his belief in her did
give her hope. What kind of seductress would she be
if she couldn't coax Heath into changing his mind?

PERSONALLY, PHOEBE FOUND the candlelight a bit too
dim—she liked to see what she was eating—but in
general, she liked the restaurant's ambience. And she
obviously wasn't alone. The place was doing a thriv-
ing Saturday-night business, making it difficult for
their harried waitress to take care of all her tables.
Heath had already observed that management didn't
have enough staff working the floor. The appetizers
had come out in a fairly timely manner, but after that
their server had disappeared. No one had brought
them refills and the wait for food was beginning to

stretch. Even with the appetizers to hold her over, Phoebe's stomach was starting to rumble.

She craned her head, scanning the crowd for their waitress. "I don't mean to sound impatient, but it would be nice if she came back some time before July."

Across the table from her, Cam smiled, his eyes twinkling as he suggested, "Maybe she got fired half-way through her shift."

Phoebe laughed at his reference. "Oh, Lord. I'd forgotten all about that dive."

"I think I'm missing something," Heath said.

Cam leaned forward, resting his arms on the table. "After Phoebe and I had been dating for a few months, she had this brilliant idea that we should stop going to decent restaurants." He put *brilliant* in air quotes.

She shot him a mock glare. "What I *said* was that we weren't very adventurous diners. So many of our friends are in the business that most places we ate, we knew the menu by heart before we even walked in the door. I suggested that maybe we should look for some hidden gems, less prestigious places that might surprise us."

"And I take it this dive you found was full of surprises?" Heath asked wryly.

"The kind of surprises the health inspector should be made aware of," Cam said, grimacing. "Phoebe's chicken nachos should have been called the salmonella special. The chicken wasn't cooked all the way through and she had to send it back. You know how softhearted she is—she *never* sends anything back."

"Then there was the margarita." Phoebe shuddered at the memory. It had been like drinking paint thinner in a salt-rimmed glass. "After two sips, I sent that back, too. As the waitress walked away, Cam's eyes bugged out. He told me he'd seen her down my entire drink. I honestly thought he was kidding."

Cam chuckled. "I *told* you I was dead serious. I don't know exactly how long we had to wait for the check, but it felt like days. I finally tracked down the manager for an explanation. Turned out, our waitress was fired on the spot for chugging Phoebe's margarita—but the guy who fired her didn't have the good sense to ask another member of the staff to cover her section. So he had six tables of angry people waiting for bills or waiting for their food. To make up for the inconvenience, he insisted we order a free dessert even though all we wanted was to get the hell out of there."

"Since we had time to kill while they got our check figured out, and I was still starving," Phoebe said, "I ordered the ice cream. I figured there was no way they could screw it up. Ten minutes later, the manager came to our table to say they'd run out." She face palmed at the memory.

"After that," Cam said, "it was a very long time before I let her choose a restaurant again."

"Oh, like you never picked any flops," Phoebe teased. "Don't you remember—" Catching sight of Heath's expression in her peripheral vision derailed her train of thought. Had anger flickered in his eyes? Probably just the candlelight. There was no way he was jealous over her reminiscing with Cam—he'd all but told her in the elevator that his goal was to help her win men over and that he wished her the best.

Still, she supposed that rehashing old times with her ex somewhat excluded Heath from the conversation. She changed the subject. "So if you go with this place, have the two of you already talked about a brand?" She knew that they wanted to do something new and suited to the area, not a duplication of Piri.

Cam nodded. "We think we've figured out something that matches the sultry nightlife vibe of the area—we just have to fine-tune the concept to make it upscale and not gimmicky."

Heath reached into his pocket for his wallet and pulled out a folded bar napkin that had the word *Hot* sketched on both sides in varying logos.

"I like this more elegant-looking one," she said, tapping the napkin. "The one in all caps with the exclamation point makes it sound like a strip club. It's a little too *Girls! Girls! Girls!*"

Heath laughed. "That's pretty much what I said, too. I like the name Hot, though. Miami doesn't seem like the place to be subtle. Cam and I are talking about focusing on spicy dishes of different heat levels—"

"We should definitely keep the jalapeño mojito on the drink menu," Cam said approvingly. He'd finished his second and had declared intentions to order a third. If their waitress ever found her way back to their table.

Heath looked around with a critical eye. "I'd like to add seating options that are more intimate—some small horseshoe booths for couples to sit side by side, maybe—but tweak the lighting and decor to make it less cliché. Miami is fun and colorful. Romantic doesn't have to be muted. We want sexy, bold touches that complement the bold menu options. And the headings could be written in a way that alludes to heat between couples."

"An appetizer section of First Impressions," Cam added. "Or a dessert menu like Afterglow or Sweet Partings." He looked a bit chagrined as he said this, as if thinking about the way he'd broken up with Phoebe and realizing it had been anything but sweet.

Had it only been this afternoon that she'd lectured him in an airport terminal about how much he'd hurt her? Tonight gave her hope that they could be friends—or at least pleasant acquaintances who moved in the same social and professional circles. She smiled across the table, about to ask him about the specific entrée ideas he had for the new restaurant when, hallelujah, the food arrived.

They were all hungry enough that conversation slowed while they ate. Unlike the dive where Phoebe and Cam had suffered through dinner so long ago, they didn't have to wait long for their check at all. It came while they were still finishing, probably because the waitress was trying to turn over the table for another group of diners. But she must have recognized Heath's name on the credit card because moments after she'd left to run the payment, the owner himself appeared at their table. He was a silver-haired man whose tie was too short for his height and whose expression was flustered.

"Mr. Jensen, Chef Pala!" He gave them a genial smile, although it didn't quite mask the nervousness in his pale eyes. "So wonderful to see you both. I didn't realize you'd be dining with us tonight."

"Well, we certainly wouldn't want to bother you during a busy weekend rush," Heath said. "Albert, meet Phoebe Mars, an up-and-coming pastry chef and my guest this evening."

Albert asked Phoebe how she'd liked her meal. The four of them talked about the restaurant business for a few minutes before he asked if they had any other plans while they were in Miami, on the pretext of suggesting local recreation. It was clear, though, that he was angling to find out if Heath and Cam had made a final decision.

In response, Heath was friendly but noncommittal, saying that their agent would be in touch. Always more focused on the culinary aspects of restaurants than the business side, Cam got into a conversation with the man about sustainable seafood and Albert invited him into the kitchen to meet the *poissonnier*.

Cam nodded eagerly, turning to make sure Heath didn't have any objections. "If the two of you don't mind, I may stick around here for a little bit, get a behind-the-scenes look."

Phoebe tried not to seem too eager to ditch him while Heath agreed that he'd meet up with his business partner in the morning. Although she'd enjoyed Cam's company tonight, she was looking forward to having Heath all to herself. Every time she recalled the scorching kiss he'd stolen, her toes curled.

They walked outside, the night air thick against her skin. Even though the sun had set, the heat was ever-present. But at the thought of being alone with him again, she shivered in happy anticipation.

"So...back to the hotel?" she asked.

His gaze dropped over her, full of masculine appreciation. "With you looking like that? It seems selfish of me to keep you cooped up in a hotel when I could show you off to Miami. Come on, Mars, let's see what kind of trouble we can get into."

As it turned out, they'd been within walking distance of a club that was popular but still accessible— it didn't garner its reputation on how many hopefuls it could turn away. Inside, they stood at a vacant high-top table. There were no chairs, but Phoebe was enjoying standing so close, leaning into Heath to better hear what he had to say over the pulsing music. He'd bought them each a glass of the establishment's signature cocktail, something rum-based, and she nursed her drink while Heath invited her to people-watch with him.

"When there's something you want to change about yourself," he said, "sometimes observing those qualities in others can be very enlightening. You see that girl in the green halter top and tight jeans making her way toward the dance floor?"

She nodded, trying to follow his lead when it came to not feeling envy.

"What's your initial impression?"

"She's...a beautiful woman who wants to dance?" Phoebe was used to being asked her opinion on culinary matters; she didn't usually spend much time speculating on strange women.

"Exactly. But one could argue she's not beautiful in the classic sense. Her features are very long. And her feet are huge. Those—"

"I'm not sure I like this side of you," Phoebe said frostily, trying not to imagine how many of her own flaws he'd tallied.

"I'm not trying to be critical," he said, backpedaling. "I was looking hard for those examples to prove a point. I think she is beautiful. But I also think physical attractiveness is at least partly how we carry ourselves. Everyone has something to be insecure about, and—"

"Ha! What could you possibly be insecure about?" She'd seen every inch of him today and *damn*. Nothing to find fault with there.

Rather than make a typically glib response, he glanced away, looking unhappy about the question. Finally, he muttered, "I was an extremely chubby kid. Some of it was baby fat that I eventually outgrew, but there was a lot of 'comfort food' after my dad died. When my mother remarried, the combo of my weight and moving to a new school made me an easy target."

She gaped. "*You* were picked on?" It was unfathomable.

"I got pretty adept at making people like me, so it didn't last long." He waved a hand as if to suggest the memories didn't bother him. "But if you ever notice my getting a little neurotic about working out, now you know why. Even godlike paragons such as myself—"

Phoebe punched him in the arm.

"—suffer from weaknesses. They don't have to hold you back if you figure out how to overcome them. I'm shit at relationships and I know it. So I've solved the problem by not having them."

She frowned, not sure that avoidance counted as a long-term solution.

But he seemed perfectly content as he added, "Hot, short-lived affairs are fun for both parties and I don't have to worry about hurting anyone—at least not in that 'I'll never trust again, God, I need a therapist' kind of way."

Had he broken someone's trust before? Or had someone betrayed his? *Probably not.* It was difficult to imagine Heath romantically invested in someone enough to trust them deeply in the first place.

"So self-acceptance," he said, pushing away his empty glass. "Very important in being seductive. Also, eye contact."

She smirked. "I could have read that little tip in any one of Gwen's magazines." Then again, seeing it in print wasn't quite the same as the sexually charged moment she and Heath had shared back in the restaurant, when he'd caught her staring at him. Wanting him.

He lifted a shoulder in a half shrug. "Truth? Most advice on how to be more seductive isn't exactly groundbreaking. A sense of humor is attractive. Who doesn't know that already? People who show they have a playful side are more fun to…play with." His lips quirked in a suggestive grin.

She grinned back, looking forward to returning to their hotel room. And making it their very own grown-up playground.

"The nice thing is that humor can be so distinctly individual, like perfume, from a subtle inside joke to an appreciation for the brash and bawdy." He rolled his eyes. "Like your roommate has."

"Gwen's not so bad. She just grew up with four siblings and learned young how to stand out in a crowd. She likes attention." She paused, realizing how little Heath discussed his past. "I can't remember—do you have siblings?"

"A stepbrother. Want another drink?"

Since hers was still half-full, she took that as a sign that he was trying to change the subject. "All right, so self-esteem, eye contact and a sense of humor. These are the secrets to making men fall at my feet?"

"Well, it helps if you can give a good blow job," he said, deadpan.

"Heath!" Her scolding tone was somewhat mitigated by her laughing aloud.

"All right, two pieces of serious advice," he said. "First, exhibiting a sense of adventure is sexy. It can be zip-lining and snorkeling with sharks or something as simple as ordering spicy food. Visit someplace you've never been, watch a scary movie. When a man sees a woman willing to try new things, it sends the subliminal message that she might be open to the idea of sex swings or threesomes with cover models. Not that most guys will ever actually do that—or that most guys know any cover models—but the power of fantasy is unbelievably compelling."

She recalled the fantasy she'd shared with him, about the stranger watching her, and her throat went dry. "Agreed." Her voice was husky and Heath gave her a knowing look. She swallowed. "Um. What was the second thing? You said there were two pieces of advice."

"More like reverse advice. I don't know what lunatic started advocating the strategy in the first place, but playing hard to get usually backfires. Being cool and aloof is the opposite of sexy. Men don't want a woman who's cold in bed. We're pretty simple—we want to be with someone who desires us and who's brazen enough to go after what she wants."

I know what I want. She'd known since before they even left the hotel.

Deciding to put his advice into action, she ran her finger over his lower lip and held his gaze with her own. "Heath? Take me back to our room and fuck me." At his shocked expression, she added a saucy smile. "Please."

8

HEATH GAVE HIMSELF an inward shake, disbelieving his own ears. Had he just experienced an auditory hallucination or had Phoebe Mars, the sweet pastry chef he habitually scandalized into blushing, actually asked him…?

"Are you sure?" he asked hoarsely.

"Very."

The reasons he'd given that afternoon for resisting temptation were nothing compared to the hungry way she was looking at him now. He grabbed her hand and began weaving through the crowd, moving toward the exit like a man on a mission. They were lucky enough to get a taxi quickly and he battled back the urge to offer the driver a fifty-dollar bill to floor it.

Instead, Heath passed the time by staring at Phoebe's legs. She'd crossed one over the other, and her split skirt revealed a silky expanse of thigh. He let go of her hand to trace idle patterns over her skin, thinking about how he wanted to touch her once they were

alone and this dress was gone. Flashes of their afternoon together tormented him: the way she'd writhed
under his tongue, the way she'd teased him in the
shower, the way she'd smiled up at him with passion-
glazed eyes.

The chemistry between them had been unques-
tionably explosive. Yet her mood tonight had left him
guessing.

When they'd left the hotel for dinner, she'd seemed
so damn glad to see Cam, beaming at him and swap-
ping all those happy memories with him. Heath had
briefly wondered if she might end their fling just as it
was beginning. But then there'd been the unexpected
gift of the way she'd looked at him while they waited
for a table. Heath had been in midsentence when he'd
felt her gaze on him like a caress. When he'd turned
toward her, there'd been so much molten heat in her
eyes that it was a wonder the fire alarm and overhead
sprinklers hadn't gone off. That moment had been the
highlight of his evening.

Correction. It was *the highlight.* Right up until
she'd looked him dead in the eye and asked him to
fuck her.

"Can't this cab go any faster?" he muttered.

Phoebe smiled, but anticipation edged her features, too.

Mercifully, the hotel was only a few blocks away
and soon the taxi was pulling up to the front entrance. Heath practically threw a handful of bills at
the driver, aware that he'd overtipped but not patient
enough to wait for change. The lobby was a blur, and

he was just glad Phoebe had no trouble keeping up with his stride in her high heels.

If they'd had the elevator to themselves, Heath knew he wouldn't have been able to refrain from touching her. But by the time the doors slid open to let them in, a small crowd had formed—a luggage-toting couple just checking in, a trio of middle-aged women and a lanky guy coming in from the pool with a towel around his neck. Everyone piled inside.

Trying to get his desire under control so that he didn't lose all finesse and pounce on her the second they reached their room, Heath avoided looking directly at Phoebe. But he was only able to hold out for a few seconds. Their gazes collided and she bit her lip, suppressing a bubble of laughter. Her eyes shone with humor as they shared the guilty secret that they were mentally undressing each other. They exited the elevator hand in hand, giggling like a couple of teenagers.

He held the door open for her and she darted into the room with a heartfelt *"Finally."*

He reached for her, but she surprised him with an evasive side step.

"Phoebe," he said sternly, "what did I tell you about playing hard to get?"

Chuckling, she went to her suitcase. "Just give me one second. You asked me if I'm sure about this? Very. This affair wasn't some spur-of-the-moment decision that I'm going to freak out about in the morning." She unzipped a section and pulled out a ridiculously large box of condoms. "See? I've given it some thought."

His voice was strangled as he held back a laugh. "Damn, woman, how many of those do you plan on us using?"

She gave him a sheepish smile. "With the wedding cake business and ordering inventory for the restaurant, I think I'm just used to buying in bulk."

"You should have warned me. Maybe I should stock up on multivitamins in the gift shop."

Rising, she tossed the box onto the nightstand, then arched one eyebrow in challenge. "Don't think you can keep up with me?"

He snagged her wrist and twirled her toward him as if they were dancing. "Let's find out," he said, his lips descending to hers as she wound her arms around his neck.

The taste of rum and Phoebe was his new favorite flavor. His mouth slanted over hers again and again, changing angles, teasing, exploring new ways to drive her crazy. Then she sucked his tongue, and he was the one in danger of coming unhinged.

Heath was no stranger to sex—the sensations pounding through his body should feel familiar, but there was no hint of déjà vu when he touched her. It was almost surreal. This was *Phoebe* pressed so tightly against him that he could feel the puckered buds of her nipples through her dress and bra. She was kissing him like she was making love to his mouth, drawing him deeper and giving him mind-blowing pleasure.

He cupped her ass and lifted her up against him, trying not to groan at the exquisite friction against his throbbing dick, then carried her to the bed. He sat on the edge with her astride him. Her skirt was bunched up around her thighs, and he could feel the heat of her against him. His fingers tightened on the lace covering her butt as she squirmed on top of him like she couldn't get close enough.

"You keep doing that," he growled with approval. "I'll sit here and enjoy the view." He kissed a path into the valley between her breasts.

She arched backward, and when he glanced up to protest her moving away, she nipped his earlobe. "Bet I can improve your view," she whispered.

Then she untied the belt at her waist and flicked open a button. The red-and-white dress pooled on the carpet in a whisper of fabric. It was difficult to say which he found sexier—the sight of her breasts covered only in dark lace or the lusty eagerness in her expression. He'd wanted Phoebe since long before he'd been willing to admit it, before she'd been available, and seeing that desire returned was a fantasy come true.

"You are so damn sexy." Crooking his fingers into the scalloped edges of her bra, he pulled the material down until her stiff pink nipples were exposed, her creamy skin framed by lace. He traced a light circle over her areola, watching the tight buds harden even more for his touch. They had that in common— he'd been hard for her since Bobbi's party. Finally, he thumbed the sensitive peak, then tugged, not watching her breasts anymore but instead fixated on the beautiful tension in her face as pleasure warred with desperate need.

A whimper caught in her throat, and Heath rolled them onto the mattress, ripping his shirt over his head right before he fell across her. Lacing his fingers through hers, he pinned her hands to the bed, leaving only his mouth free to worship her breasts. He moved slightly to the side, his thigh between her legs, and propped himself up as he sucked and nibbled and teased. She responded with fevered abandon, gyrating against him until his pants were damp from her.

Tiny beads of perspiration dotted her skin, and the combined salty tang of their sweaty bodies reminded him of the ocean, if the ocean was hot to the touch. And right now, he wanted to submerge himself in her slick depths.

He raised himself up on an elbow to kiss her again before impatiently shucking his pants and boxer briefs. Phoebe glanced down, eyeing him with greedy enthusiasm as a smile curved her lips. He reached for the box of condoms that had so amused him earlier. As aroused as he was right now, it was difficult to remember why the idea of making love to her a dozen times a day had ever seemed funny.

She wriggled out of her panties while he opened one square packet, and then held out her hand. "Let me," she said. She unrolled the condom over his length, and he had to grit his teeth at the tantalizing pressure of her hand and the urge to thrust against her.

When she finished, she laid back down next to

him, trailing her fingers over his cheek. "I want you so much."

The soft words seemed like the sweetest he'd ever heard. Kissing her deeply, he laid across her, pressed against her entrance. She was so wet, there was no question that she was ready for him, but he slid inside her as slowly as he could, savoring the moment. Savoring her. "God, Phoebe. You feel so good."

He rolled his hips, stirring inside her, and she moaned, tightening around him. When he leaned down to take her nipple in his mouth, she squeezed him even harder. He flexed forward, losing himself in her, increasing his pace, urged on by the way her legs were locked around him and her fingernails raked his back. Sensations blurred together as they moved more frantically, the slide of her skin against his, the rich, womanly scent of her, the sexy sounds she made.

She licked the side of his neck while he worked his hand between them, finding her clit just long enough for Phoebe's cries to change from soft, breathy hums of enjoyment to a near shout. She arched her back off the mattress, her muscles clenching around him, and he watched as her climax took her. She was breathing hard, her eyes closed, one arm pressed against the wall behind her as she bucked her hips. His own orgasm started to build and he moved with mindless purpose, in and out of her as she smiled up at him, her expression radiating pure bliss. That smile sent him over the edge and he was coming in waves that racked his entire body.

He more or less collapsed afterward, dazed by how

perfect that had been. He turned his head on his pillow, not sure what to say to her, which was a first. Everything that came to mind seemed either too glib or trite.

Phoebe's brow wrinkled as she stared back at him. "You look...nervous?"

"Maybe I am." It seemed as good a word as any to describe the strange, fluttery feeling in the pit of his stomach.

She chuckled. "Shouldn't the performance anxiety come *before* the sex? Not that you have anything to be anxious about. That was amazing."

"I just don't want this to change anything," he said softly. With a couple of rare exceptions, after he'd had sex with someone a few times, the woman stopped being part of his life. But he couldn't stand the thought of going weeks without seeing Phoebe, without glimpsing her smile or hearing her scold him for outrageous behavior.

Her expression shifted, and she rolled to the side of the bed. "Of course it didn't change anything. Don't worry, you were very clear—this is a vacation fling. Not real life." Then she rose and went into the bathroom.

He watched her go, the jittery feeling inside unabated. If nothing had changed, why did he feel irrevocably altered?

Mmm. By nature, Phoebe was a person who clung to sleep as long as she could. The snooze button on her alarm clock was probably dented, and she doubted she'd ever awakened with a smile on her face. But the lean masculine body and steely erection pressed against her provided a far more enjoyable wake-up than any alarm. She and Heath were laying on their sides, him spooning her while cupping one breast possessively.

Languid heat wound through her, increasing exponentially when he began to trace slow circles over her breast until the peak was rigid and begging for attention. He brushed his thumb over her nipple, then pinched, making her gasp. She'd barely opened her eyes yet, and she was already dripping wet for him.

He slid her hair to the side so that he could kiss the back of her neck. "Mornin'," he murmured against her skin.

Best morning ever, she decided as he reached down and caressed her between her legs. He placed a hand on her shoulder, pushing lightly until she rolled onto her stomach, then he trailed kisses across her spine, making her tremble.

"You have such a great ass," he told her with an affectionate swat before reaching for the condoms on the nightstand. After he put one on, he lowered his weight against her, his voice a dark temptation in her ear. "Are you awake enough to get on your hands and knees?"

Her breath caught, and she nodded enthusiastically. This wasn't a position she had much experience with, and the novelty was an added thrill—which was saying something given how thrilling sex with Heath already was. She did experience half a second's insecurity when she realized her butt was completely on display to him, wishing she'd made more time for toning yoga classes, but Heath clearly enjoyed her generous curves.

She couldn't resist looking back over her shoulder at the erotic sight of him positioning himself at her entrance, imagining what the view was like from his angle, the anticipation he felt. He gripped her hips and thrust forward, driving into her.

"Oh," she breathed as he withdrew just long enough to repeat the motion and bury himself inside her again. Last night had been fantastic, but in this position he seemed even deeper, hitting a spot she hadn't known… "Oh, my *God*."

She eagerly rocked back to meet him, her eyes closed as sensation spread through her. He moved with more force, their bodies slapping together in an increasingly frenzied rhythm. Heath's grip on her was just shy of bruising. Funny how, with him holding her so tightly, she felt so free. Rapturous.

As she reached a place where she felt almost outside herself, her climax hit in spasms of pleasure that radiated through her whole body. Her muscles clenched around him and he slammed into her one last time with a hoarse shout, then they both fell forward onto the pillows. He cuddled her against his chest, and she listened to his heart racing beneath her cheek.

It took her a few minutes to collect her thoughts, but when she did, she snickered softly. *Well, that's one way to avoid the "haven't brushed my teeth yet" problem of morning sex.*

PHOEBE HAD A fleeting recollection of Heath asking if she wanted to join him in the shower. She wasn't sure if she'd actually muttered, "Rain check" before falling back asleep, or if she'd only thought it. But in what seemed like a blink of an eye, he'd gone from naked and snuggling with her to standing next to the bed in a suit, smelling like expensive soap.

"Sharp-dressed man," she said around a yawn. "Sorry I drifted off instead of helping you wash your back."

"Don't be." He leaned down to kiss her cheek. "As it is, I'm running a few minutes late. If you'd been in the shower with me, there's a high probability I would have been distracted."

She sat up, keeping the sheet over her breasts so as not to distract him. "Thank you for this morning. That was better than coffee."

He grinned. "High praise. I just wish I could stay and laze in bed with you." His expression turned regretful as he headed toward the door. "If you don't have any plans today, there's a spa here at the hotel. You could get a massage or something."

A week ago, that probably would have struck her as a good idea. But what was the point in paying someone to make her body feel good when Heath had already accomplished that so thoroughly?

"Actually, I think I want to see the Wynwood Walls." The collection of warehouses had become a canvas for amazing street art and murals, with an international assortment of artists contributing. "And

I'll grab lunch at the farmer's market I'm visiting. You'll be busy until this evening, right?"

He made a face. "Three meetings—wait, four including the bank—and a scouting expedition just in case something goes south with Albert's restaurant and we have to get serious about our backup location. If only I could let Cam take the business stuff for a day and play hooky. But he can barely stay awake when Miranda's going through all the tenant legalese."

Ah, yes, Heath had a breakfast meeting with the lovely agent who was "smitten" with him. *And I am not jealous.* Phoebe was a mature adult who'd gone into this affair with her eyes open, aware that neither she nor Heath had any lasting hold on the other.

Giving him a blithe smile, she raised her arms over her head in a stretch and let the sheet fall away from her torso.

His avid gaze zeroed in on her bare breasts, and he sucked in his breath. "Evil, evil tease."

She blew him a kiss. "Just something to remember me by when you're stuck in all those boring meetings."

"Maybe I can rush through a few of them. I mean, how important are contract clauses and property maintenance, really?"

When he took a half step toward her, she laughed in protest. "Go! I don't want to single-handedly torpedo your new restaurant before it's even up and running."

"All right, I'm out of here. But maybe you should

get a little more rest before you start sightseeing." He gave her a smile full of predatory promise. "You're going to need your energy later."

9

EVEN IF HEATH hadn't been irritated as hell with both of his companions, he still wouldn't want to be trapped in this cozy, tropically decorated meeting room with them. The ceiling fan spinning lazily overhead was no substitute for the fresh air he could be enjoying with Phoebe right now. He wanted to stroll through the farmer's market with her, take her for a long walk down a secluded stretch of beach and see if he could coax her into getting good and sandy with him. Instead, he was stuck in this pastel-walled office with his increasingly snide business partner and a flirtatious leasing agent.

Miranda Lima was a very attractive woman—she was statuesque with jet-black hair and almond eyes, and her quick intellect made her even more appealing. In the past, Heath had been flattered by her extrabright smiles and personal attention. But…was it his imagination, or was she coming on aggressively strong today? Even the way she'd offered him coffee had sounded like an innuendo. He was reminded of the night he'd cooked Phoebe dinner in his loft. *How do you make it sound like you're thinking about sex all the time?*

Dammit, did *he* usually sound to others the way Miranda had seemed to him when she'd greeted him today? Grating and pushy?

"Heath?" Miranda's expression wasn't coquettish now. Instead, she looked annoyed. "You don't have any opinion on the exclusivity clause?"

Exclusivity in restaurant leases helped guarantee that a place with the exact same concept didn't open next door. It protected their business model and prevented the most egregious forms of competition. Part of Miranda's job was also making sure they weren't violating anyone else's clause with their location and idea.

Seated in the padded wicker chair next to Heath, Cam snorted. "Being exclusive isn't really Heath's forte. He's more a…free-market guy."

Heath cut a glare in his partner's direction. He was used to Cam not being a lot of help at these meetings, but today was the first time he'd been actively sarcastic. "Sorry, Miranda. I guess I'm not at my sharpest this morning. Is it too late to take you up on that offer of coffee?"

She frowned but managed to sound gracious when she replied, "Never too late for my favorite client. Besides, I could use a refill, too." She rose from her chair. "Cameron?"

"No, thank you."

As soon as she was gone from the room, Heath confronted his associate in an angry whisper. "What the hell is your problem this morning?"

"My problem? I'm not the one who keeps spacing out during key points of negotiation. What's the matter, Jensen? Not enough sleep last night?" Cam asked, his tone abnormally caustic.

Then it clicked. "This is about Phoebe. You're mad because she and I spent the night together?" Cameron would be even more pissed if he had the first inkling what had happened there. Studying the man's pinched features and bloodshot eyes, Heath reconsidered. Cam probably had a pretty good guess.

Cam didn't deny his jealousy. "She and I weren't even apart for two weeks before you swooped in!"

"You're the one who broke up with her, jackass." Heath fought hard to keep his voice down so that they didn't draw attention from the outer office. "If you'd nurtured your relationship, there wouldn't have been any swooping."

"Are you sure about that?" Cam challenged.

That hit close to home. "I have *never* made a move on a woman in a relationship."

"Because the two of you seem awfully close, awfully fast. Can you honestly look me in the eye and tell me that you didn't want her before our fight?"

"It wasn't a fight, Cameron, you *dumped* her."

"And that's not an answer to my question." Cam stood, fists clenched at his sides. "Or maybe the fact that you won't give me an answer tells me all I need to know. You wanted her, didn't you? And as soon as I made a mistake, you were conveniently there as her shoulder to cry on."

Heath faltered, recalling how stricken she'd looked at Bobbi's party to see Cam with a date—and how he had taken advantage of the situation to kiss her for the first time.

Cam gave him a withering look. "Christ, Jensen, you've dated half the women in Atlanta. You really had to add the woman I love to the list?"

"If you loved her—"

"I screwed up! You don't think I know that?" Cameron was breathing hard, not even attempting to keep his voice at a civil volume. "I think I'll go for a walk. Text me before we have to head to the bank. You and Miranda can finish up here. She barely notices I'm in the room anyway."

Heath took a deep breath. "Can we be professional about this?"

Genuine hurt flashed in the man's dark eyes. "Sorry, this feels personal. I don't even care that our friendship meant so little to you that you pounced the minute you saw an opportunity. But I do care about Phoebe. She deserves better than your typical 'love 'em and leave 'em' tactics."

I care about her, too. The words hovered on the tip of his tongue. He wanted to argue that she was special, different. But how could he claim that when he was treating their fling like so many others he'd had over the past few years? Just temporary fun. He'd known that sleeping with her was a dicey line to cross, but it hadn't taken much persuading to get him to sprint over it. Not that he would take back last night—or this morning—even if he could.

Was Cam right, then? Right about Heath's selfishness and the likelihood of his hurting Phoebe?

He tried to assuage his conscience with the reminder that last night had been her idea. She fully understood that he wasn't offering anything lasting. And it had been Phoebe who called him in the first place to ask for help with her seduction skills and to prove a point to Cam. *After you put the idea in her head.*

Heath had a pretty lenient ethical code when it came to his sex life, but he'd assured himself more than once that he was morally superior to the stepbrother who'd stolen the woman Heath loved. Now he was less sure. Even if he'd denied it to himself at the time, he'd wanted Phoebe for months. He'd seen the sexy woman buttoned into the chef's jacket. He'd loved teasing her and chatting baseball with her and seeking her opinion on everything from restaurant tablecloths to what to buy people for their birthdays. Getting a blush and chiding smile from her had become something of a daily goal.

I'm a bastard. He'd betrayed his partnership with Cam by coveting his girlfriend, and he hadn't dealt fairly with Phoebe, either. What had he said to her at Bobbi's birthday? *Do you trust me?* Ha! He and his ulterior motives had convinced her to fly across state lines, where he could seduce her without her overprotective roommate giving him the kick to the balls he probably deserved.

"Wait!" Heath called after Cameron as he reached

the doorway. "We're still able to work together, right?" It was easier to worry about the new restaurant than to worry about whether he'd taken advantage of one of his closest friends.

Cam sighed. "Phoebe is a grown woman, free to make her own choices. If she wants you, I'll be a mature adult about it—even though we both know you'll break her heart before the summer's even over."

No, that wouldn't happen. He and Phoebe had agreed that hearts wouldn't be involved. But it seemed crass to tell Cameron everything between them was purely sexual.

"I want the same respect from you, Jensen." Cam jabbed a finger at him. "If she picks me, if she decides to rekindle what we had, you step aside gracefully."

No. Every fiber of his being rebelled at the idea of her back in Cam's arms. Which was the height of self-absorbed pettiness. If his affair with Phoebe was limited only to a few days in Miami, then he had no claim on her past this trip.

So he'd better make their time together count for all it was worth.

IT WAS DIFFICULT to say which was the more colorful venue: the artfully graffitied warehouse walls Phoebe had visited earlier or the farmer's market where she was browsing. She'd passed by a number of food vendors and a mariachi band outside and made her way into the huge building that held bin after bin of fresh produce. The structure was a cross between a greenhouse and a barn, with lots of light shining in, and the countless rows of fruits and vegetables were a riot of red, yellow, green, purple and other hues. Among the more common bananas and oranges were palm fruit, bumpy green atemoya and bitter melon. She stopped to try a sample of deep orange mamey, which had an indescribable flavor that reminded her of half a dozen things at once, from carrot to honeydew.

She could only imagine what it would be like to come here with Heath, exchanging bites of the creamy fruit or sharing a glass of guava juice. The farmer's market was already a banquet for the senses, but she'd noticed that when she was in Heath's company, everything seemed heightened somehow. Her physical awareness of him was so acute that it magnified sights, sounds and tastes.

And when this passionate liaison is over? What then—everything becomes muted and vanilla? Couldn't she just worry about that next week? Last night, after she'd propositioned him, she'd decided to view these next few days as a criminally rich dessert—something that wasn't good for her at all in the long run, but offered too much short-term bliss not to sample. She'd told Heath she wouldn't regret having sex with him.

And she didn't regret it. Everything they'd done together had been phenomenal. It was just that, since arriving in Miami, this was the first time she'd been alone to process all that had happened. Without Heath at her side, her hormones weren't clamoring quite so loudly and she could hear other thoughts creeping in. Skeptical, fretting thoughts.

With a sigh, she reminded herself that she was here as a foodie, not as a neurotic girlfriend obsessing over a guy. She turned away from the fruit stand and rounded the aisle, walking up a new row. White sacks full of pungent spices and dried peppers lined the wall…which made her think of Heath again. *Not because you're pathetic. The guy's opening a restaurant called Hot.* Of course *you're going to be reminded of him when eyeing a load of habaneros.*

She made her way into an adjoining building that featured a bakery counter full of local specialties, like *turrones* and colorful pan dulce shaped like sea shells and pound cake with guava marmalade. It all looked delicious, but for once in her life, she didn't want any dessert.

What she really wanted right now was to talk to Gwen.

Her roommate had been her best friend for over a decade, the person Phoebe had confided in about everything from her first kiss to slow dancing at the prom to losing her virginity in college. Though Phoebe had never been quite as free with the details as Gwen usually was, she at least wanted to tell her friend how incredible last night and this morning had been. Maybe it would be easier to silence the whisper of doubts if she could share her happiness with someone.

Assuming Gwen would even be happy for me. Her bestie had been pretty vocal about Heath's reputation. She was not a fan. Besides, Gwen was probably on set right now anyway. She could hardly chat about

Phoebe's sex life while giving one of Hollywood's most popular young starlets fangs and vampire eyes.

Phoebe walked back outside to evaluate her lunch options. There were several food trucks parked on the periphery, and they made her chuckle, reminding her of Cam's occasional declarations that he was going to pack up his knives and hit the open culinary road. The year that Piri had opened, she'd thought that Cam was very focused, which she'd respected. Her entire adolescence had been focused on leaving home and what she wanted to do with her life once she did. And although she'd held several different jobs in the past few years, she'd been steadily building her own business, which she hoped would be self-sustaining within the next five years. It was only in retrospect that she realized much of Cam's seeming concentration came from Heath keeping him on track.

Truthfully, Cam was indecisive. He vacillated on everything from monthly menus to his love life, convincing himself that Phoebe hadn't been enough to make him happy and now acting as if he missed her. In contrast, Heath lived life deliberately. Some people might look at his dating patterns and think that he just hadn't found the right partner. But a person didn't accidentally date eleven women in a month. He'd admitted as much last night, saying that his no-strings lifestyle was a conscious choice. Phoebe needed to keep that in mind.

It was okay to get temporarily swept away by her craving for him, just so long as she didn't let it sweep her into delusion.

She purchased a couple of tamales and a bottle of ice-cold water, then made her way to a shaded picnic table. As she was setting down her lunch, the phone in her pocket vibrated and she had an unrealistic flare of optimism that Heath might have concluded his business hours ahead of schedule. But when she pulled out her phone, she was thrilled to see Gwen's name on the screen.

"Hey!" She sat on the bench, grinning from ear to ear. "You must be psychic. I was thinking a couple of minutes ago about how much I wanted to talk to you."

"Best-friend ESP," Gwen said sagely. "Our connection is a finely tuned vibration in the universe, and— Nah. I was calling to gush about this stand-in I intend to jump who's even hotter than the actor he's blocking for. So, Gwen sexy times. The usual."

They both chuckled, but before Phoebe could respond, her friend's tone turned serious.

"I also called because I owe you an apology," Gwen said unexpectedly. "You know who I ran into yesterday? Alisha Tulloch, one of Heath's former playmates."

Phoebe tensed. Was this going to evolve into a legitimate apology, or was Gwen working up to a bait and switch where she once again explained why Phoebe shouldn't sleep with Heath? Because it was a little late for that lecture.

"I remember Alisha," Phoebe said cautiously. She was a high-powered attorney, unaccustomed to losing. That breakup had been one of Heath's more memorable because Alisha had been convinced she could wear him down if she kept arguing her case. To demonstrate his resolve, Heath had finally threatened to ban her from Piri.

"Yeah, well, she's engaged now."

"Wow, that was fast."

"They've been together four months and Alisha claims love at first sight. I saw them together and, for a brilliant, successful woman…" Gwen gave a low whistle. "She is hella clingy. It didn't seem to bother her fiancé, but I found myself thinking that if I'd been Heath, I would have kicked her to the curb, too. Maybe I've been too hard on him. After all, it's not like *I'm* the poster girl for monogamy, right?"

Phoebe actually pulled the phone away from her ear and stared at it, as if searching for clues that this was a high-tech prank. "Who are you and what have you done with Gwendolyn Yeager?"

"Regardless of what I think of Heath, I should have been more supportive of you." Gwen's voice was laden with remorse. "I know better than anyone how you were raised, how you were basically taught to feel ashamed for any physical impulse you might have. It occurred to me while I was making plans to jump the hot new stand-in that you're entitled to some sexy times, too. Who deserves it more than you? Go forth and boink with my blessing. Not that you need it—you're a consenting adult—but I wanted to offer it anyway."

Phoebe smiled, filled with affection for her friend. "Go forth and boink" wasn't the most poignant sentiment, but Phoebe found the words oddly touching.

"Thank you. I may not need your permission, but I do need your friendship. You mean the world to me."

"Are you grateful enough for my friendship that you're willing to share lurid details? Because it occurs to me, the number of infatuated lovers must mean Jensen is doing something right in bed."

"Many, many things." Phoebe sighed happily.

"Spill!"

"Um…" Her cheeks heated as she recalled their fiercely carnal encounter that morning. She darted her glance around at the couple dozen people in the area. "You'll just have to use your imagination."

"That's not— Oh, crap, they need me for touch-ups. Gotta go! But we aren't finished with this conversation."

By the time Phoebe's phone rang again, she had returned to her hotel room and was trying to decide whether to change into her new bikini and go for a swim, or read a book on the balcony and enjoy the breeze and the gorgeous beach view. This time, the caller was Heath and she flopped across the bed to answer, bending her knees and kicking her feet up behind her the way she used to do when she and Gwen talked on the phone as teenagers.

"Whatcha wearing?" he asked.

A turquoise sundress that tied behind her neck. "My smile and a pair of stilettos."

There was a charged silence as he processed that answer. "Damn, woman, are you trying to kill me?"

"Of course not—I'm not finished having my way with you yet."

His response was half laugh, half groan. "I've created a very sexy monster."

"Are you calling to tell me you'll be back to the hotel soon?" Her pulse accelerated, and she resisted the urge to snuggle with his pillow and see if she could detect his scent on it. "I'll make a list of monstrous things I want to do to you when you get here."

He groaned. "Oh, how I wish I was headed back to you. Unfortunately we're doing our complete examination of Albert's books, and everything has taken longer than it should have today. Cam— Well, never mind about Cam. We're going to have a working dinner, but it should be early, maybe five thirty or six? I'll be back after that. Tomorrow I have more free time to spend with you," he said apologetically, "and we have the ballgame on Tuesday. But for this evening, I'm afraid you're on your own for dinner."

"No problem. There are plenty of food options at the hotel."

"Just promise me something," he said.

"What's that?"

"Save room for dessert."

A PEAL OF laughter escaped Phoebe when Heath carried two small coolers into the room. A uniformed hotel employee followed behind with a room service cart that included a stack of small plates, utensils and chilled champagne in a bucket of ice.

After tipping the man, Heath looked back in her direction. "What's so funny?"

"I just realized you were being literal," she admitted. "When you mentioned dessert earlier, I kind of thought it was a euphemism."

A slow smile spread across his face. "Why, Phoebe Mars, you have a dirty mind. Nice to see I've corrupted you. But no, I actually need your opinion. Not only are Cam and I working on the potential menu for the new restaurant, we're auditioning potential employees. I brought back a variety of tasting-size samples and thought we could enjoy them on the balcony and watch the sunset. Want to open the champagne while I change?"

She laughed. "Isn't slipping into something more comfortable the woman's line?"

"Good point." A devilish gleam entered his eyes as he studied her loose-flowing maxidress. "That looks terribly constricting. You should take it off."

Tempting. "If I do that, we'll miss the sunset. And what about dessert?"

"Who needs dessert when I have you?" He took a step toward her, then paused. "Although, to be perfectly honest, there are a few things in those coolers that will melt if we don't get to them."

She made shooing motions. "Go change. We can revisit how binding my dress is later."

When he went around the corner to the bathroom, she opened the sliding glass door and wheeled the cart out between the two padded chairs that sat on the balcony. It was a very romantic setting. An evening breeze was coming from the water, leaving the night sultry but bearable. Red and orange streaked the darkening sky. The desserts deserved an equally picturesque presentation. Rather than eat them out of take-out containers, she took the small stack of dishes room service had delivered and made a circle. Then she began plating the selections. The first cooler included truffles, pomegranate mousse, dark chocolate wasabi bark, cream-filled pastries and watermelon mint sorbet.

Catching sight of the sorbet, she was suddenly reminded of an article she'd glimpsed in one of Gwen's magazines. She'd forgotten all about it, not thinking to include it when Heath had asked about her fantasies, but now she was intrigued.

She glanced around, checking the balcony's privacy. The terraces were staggered so that a person had to stand at the very edge and peer around the corner to see onto a neighbor's, and the high concrete safety ledge afforded a bit of seclusion. Her lips curved in anticipation. When she'd first come outside, she'd noted that the breeze was keeping the heat at bay. But the night was about to get a whole lot hotter.

HEATH STEPPED OUT into the fading light, dressed in a pair of linen shorts and a rayon shirt he hadn't bothered to button. The casual clothes were comfortable but he was regretting suggesting the balcony instead of feeding each other the desserts while naked in bed.

He grinned at the professional arrangement of desserts on the table. *Ever the pastry chef.* It all looked wonderful, but the redhead handing him a flute of champagne was the most delectable of all.

"Quite a selection," she said.

"I felt bad that we couldn't have dinner together." Heath had always loved the challenges of his work— the long hours usually felt more like a familiar refuge than a dreaded inconvenience. But this afternoon, not even the excitement of opening a new restaurant had been able to keep his mind off Phoebe. "Providing dessert was the least I could do."

She picked up one of the small square plates. "Do you like pomegranate?" At his nod, she dipped a finger into the mousse and held it up for him. "It's rumored to be an aphrodisiac."

As far as he was concerned, there was no more powerful aphrodisiac than her smile, but he raised her finger to his lips, swiping his tongue over it for a quick taste before sucking it clean. Her eyelids fluttered, and she gave a soft sigh of pleasure. To hell with the desserts. He wanted to lay her across the rolling table and sample her until he'd wrung a dozen more sighs from her.

Then she kissed him, leisurely exploring his mouth before pulling away to grin up at him. "Tart. I like it."

He leaned into her so that she could feel his growing erection. "Guess its aphrodisiac qualities are legit."

She palmed his hardness through the shorts, giving him a look of mock pity. "Poor Heath. These bottoms seem to be very constricting." Then she surprised him by deftly undoing the drawstring and sliding the shorts down in one fluid motion.

He stepped out of them and pitched them onto the chair behind him.

Phoebe trailed her fingers over the fly of his boxer briefs in a maddeningly light touch. "These, too."

All he was left with was an unbuttoned shirt, while she was fully dressed. "This isn't going how I imagined," he said wryly. "One of us is overdressed."

"Give me five minutes," she said seductively, her eyes flashing mischief, "and I bet you won't be complaining. Have a seat."

He sat in the chair, not entirely sure what she was planning but willing to follow her lead. Especially when she pulled the cushion off the other chair and set it at his feet, nudging his thighs apart.

"Next up is the watermelon-mint sorbet," she told him. She bent at the waist to offer him a spoonful, her long hair tickling across his lap.

He couldn't think about menu options right now. Or about anything, really. All the blood in his brain was rushing south. But he obligingly tasted the sorbet. "Nice." The bite of mint kept it from being too sweet—much like Phoebe, who, for all her sweetness, had a lot of hidden zing.

She sank to her knees on the cushion, her fingers tracing figure eights over his thighs. "I thought of something I want to add to my fucket list."

"Really?" His voice caught as she gripped his shaft. "Because, I gotta be honest, this seems more like *my* fantasy."

Smiling, she held his gaze as she bent down, not breaking contact until the very last minute when she licked across the tip of him. Then she ran her tongue along the ridge encircling the head. Sensation shivered up his spine, and he gripped the arms of the chair. Hard.

All too soon, she rocked back on her heels and he considered begging for more. She shot him a wicked smile and picked up the sorbet again, taking a spoonful into her mouth before lowering her head. This time she didn't stop with gentle licks. She closed her lips over him and sucked. The jolt of cold made him gasp, but almost immediately he felt tingles of pleasure as she slid along his length, her mouth and hand tight around him.

She repeated the sorbet trick two more times, then increased the suction around him while he tangled his hands in her hair, babbling fragments of praise and curse words and her name. It felt so fucking *good* that he hated for it to end, even as he knew he couldn't hold out much longer, not against this onslaught of ecstasy. She was swirling her tongue around him while pumping him with her hand, and he caught his breath long enough to warn her.

"I'm so close. I'm about to—"

She tightened her hold on him and brushed her hair over her shoulder, giving him a good look at her while her head bobbed along his shaft, and then it was all over. His hips came off the chair and there was a roaring in his ears and it felt like it went on forever. Afterward, he rested his head against the back of his chair, wondering if he would ever recover and not really caring if he didn't. Either way, it had been worth it. She gave him one last affectionate lick, then reached for her flute of champagne.

"So." She sipped her drink, then flashed him a smile over the rim. "Think you'll put watermelon-mint sorbet on the menu?"

"Hell, no. Every time I saw it, I'd be too hard to walk straight." He wiggled his toes, testing to see if he still had full use of his limbs. When she passed him his own glass of champagne, he drained the contents. Then he slowly stood. "I think we should go inside now."

She glanced at the desserts they'd yet to try. "Are we done?"

"Not at all." He picked up the plate of éclairs and cream puffs with some very definite ideas about licking chocolate and cinnamon custard off her skin. "We're just getting started."

PHOEBE CRACKED ONE eye open, looking to see if there was any water left in the bottle on the nightstand, then came fully awake when she saw the clock. "Holy crap! What time are we supposed to meet Cam downstairs?" Any thorough restaurant evaluation included both weekend and weekday visits, as well as an idea of the area's traffic flow at different times of the day. They'd made plans for an early lunch.

Next to her, Heath snuggled deeper under the comforter and mumbled something unintelligible.

She jabbed him in the shoulder. "Time to look alive, Jensen. It's almost eleven."

That got his attention. He sat bolt upright. "Are you messing with me? We're supposed to be downstairs in fifteen minutes." He grabbed his phone off the other nightstand. "I could have sworn I set—oh, here's the problem. Nine p.m."

"A.m. might have worked better," she teased. "Alarm or no alarm, I can't believe I slept so long." When was the last time she'd stayed in bed this late? Then again, she rarely had such a compelling reason to be in bed as the man beside her. "You obviously exhausted me, keeping me awake all night."

His lips curled in a satisfied smile, and he looked ridiculously sexy for a man with bed head and stubble. "You don't expect me to apologize for our active night, do you? I mean, I can. But it would be insincere as hell."

She grinned back at him. "I don't want an apology, just coffee. Can you brew some while I jump in the shower?"

He waggled his eyebrows at her. "I have a better idea."

"No! Any more of your ideas and we won't make it out of here in time for dinner, much less lunch."

"Why say that like it's a bad thing? The hotel has room service."

Chuckling, she climbed out of bed, wearing only the T-shirt of his she'd pulled on around five o'clock in the morning because he'd stolen the blankets. She could feel his gaze on her as she scooped clothes out of her suitcase.

"You should just keep that shirt," he said. "It's never going to look as good on me as it does on you."

She froze, startled by the words. Keeping something—even an old cotton shirt—sounded so permanent, so the opposite of what they'd agreed on. Was it Heath's way of preparing for goodbye, giving her a memento of the time they'd had together? *A parting gift.* Or did it mean something else?

It's a damn shirt, Pheeb. Stop overanalyzing and get in the shower.

She went into the bathroom, but being in a rush to beat the clock only heightened her awareness of how fast their time in Miami was running out. Soon she'd be back to her life—a job she loved, the world's kindest boss, a roommate who always made her laugh, new cake orders she'd accepted by email while she was here. All good things.

Yet the thought of getting on that plane the day after tomorrow stung.

On Thursday morning, she would wake up in her bed, alone. Without Heath to kiss her or tease her or even steal the blankets. Her throat tightened at the realization of how much she would miss him, and she tried to blink away the burn in her eyes.

Not waking up next to him wouldn't even be the worst part. There was no diplomatic way to ask how long he thought he'd wait until he fell into some other woman's bed. How soon would Phoebe have to face him with his arm around some stunning date? *You knew what you were getting into. You promised yourself, promised him, that you could handle this.*

All true.

Then again, she'd been wrong about her love life before.

10

LUNCH HELPED CURE Phoebe's brief bout of melancholy; it was difficult to mope when you were eating delicious food. While Cam ordered an entrée off the menu, she and Heath had both chosen the buffet. Although Heath respectfully refrained from any innuendos about how he'd worked up his appetite, he did wink at her as he went back for a third visit to the seafood bar.

Being left alone with Cam at the table made Phoebe feel self-conscious. Even though she didn't owe him anything now that they were split up—and she very much doubted he'd been celibate for the past month—it was strange to be sitting with her ex after everything she'd done with his business partner in the past twelve hours.

She cleared her throat. "So, um, I take it the jury's in and this will be the site of the new restaurant?"

"There are some details to finalize, but yeah, looks that way. It's a good place with a lot of potential."

She nodded. "I've certainly enjoyed being here."

"I've enjoyed you being here, too," he told her earnestly. "Phoebe, the past couple of days have been a revelation. You've changed." His admiring gaze made it clear the words were intended as a compliment.

Yet she found herself annoyed. He obviously liked what he saw—*now*. Where had that admiration been when she was just plain Phoebe, before the enhanced cleavage and makeup and rosy aura of sexual afterglow? She tried to return his smile rather than glare, but abandoned the effort in favor of viciously spearing her seared tuna.

Obviously unaware that he was skipping through a field of emotional land mines, Cam added, "You look beautiful today."

"Thanks." With so little time to get ready, there'd been no chance to dry her hair. She'd simply braided it in a thick rope, impressing herself with the makeup application she'd managed in five minutes. Gwen would be proud.

"Really beautiful," he said firmly.

She mentally rolled her eyes. *I heard you the first time.* Logically, she realized she was being a hypocrite. What kind of person set out to be more exciting and seductive, then got irritated when people responded to those very qualities? *You're the one who wanted a makeover.*

But had she really *wanted* one, for her own sake? Or had it been a knee-jerk reaction to getting dumped and feeling as if she was inadequate? Whatever the motivation, Cam certainly appreciated the results.

And he wasn't the only one. Heath, who was used to being surrounded by beautiful, accomplished women, had been looking at her for the past few days as if she was a goddess. He not only appreciated her evolution, but he'd also partially engineered it. On the phone yesterday, he'd told her he'd created a sexy monster. Last night, happy to have "corrupted" her, he'd taken credit for her dirty mind. From the moment she'd asked for his help, he'd been making her feel sexier and more sophisticated. Actually, the transformation from demure, well-behaved Phoebe had begun even before she'd called him.

It had been sparked when he unexpectedly kissed her, when she'd shown up at Bobbi's party looking not like pastry chef Phoebe Mars, but a Bond-girl version of herself from an alternate reality. One of the very first things Heath had commented on that night was how different she looked. Obviously, different was good. If Gwen hadn't sent her out of the house in that low-cut dress and those killer shoes, would Phoebe even be here in Miami right now?

The question stabbed at her. As much as she enjoyed being sexy for Heath, it was somewhat deflating to feel as though he was more attracted to the fantasy illusion of herself than the real person.

Why does it even matter?

The end result was the same. Regardless of what had first caught his attention—whether it was her roommate's borrowed stilettos, or Phoebe's "graceful" neck or, hell, the scent of her body wash—the past few days had been incredible. Besides, it would

be one thing if they were trying to build a relationship and she questioned whether their foundation was
strong enough, more than superficial attraction. But
this wasn't a relationship. It was exhilarating sex, an
affair that would be over forty-eight hours from now.

So stop obsessing over the whys and wherefores.
She was supposed to be confident and seductive, not
neurotic.

Later, once she'd gone back to her regularly scheduled life, she could examine whether or not she really
wanted to change to impress a man, or if she was content with who she was. In the meantime, she was the
focus of Heath Jensen's sensual attention. Why not
create as many memorable experiences as possible?

Phoebe tied the sarong skirt at her hip, not that the
filmy white material actually hid anything from view.
If she'd realized sooner that Heath and Cam were
going to brainstorm menu options for Hot at the hotel
pool, maybe she wouldn't have made that second trip
to the buffet.

Nonsense. This vacation was about indulgence, not
deprivation. And even if she wasn't used to showing
as much skin as the ice-blue bikini revealed, she had
to admit that her reflection looked pretty damn good.
She recalled the night in Heath's loft, and her lips
curved—she'd improved substantially at appreciating the babe in the mirror. Sliding on a pair of black
sunglasses, she exited the bathroom.

"All ready," she told Heath. He was in black swim
trunks and the same shirt he'd thrown on last night

for their dessert tasting. Remembering the hours that had followed left her skin flushed; it wouldn't take much for the twinge of desire she felt to bloom into something more all consuming. With Heath in the room, it never did.

He grinned. "Want me to rub sunscreen on you? I promise to be very thorough."

"I'll bet."

He gave her a stern look. "Protection from UV rays is a serious matter, Mars."

Yeah, something a pale redhead who burned easily had known since preschool. "Which is why I've already applied plenty of sunblock." She paused a beat, then flashed a sly smile. "Although...I may have missed a spot on my back. Maybe you can help me when we get down to the pool?"

"I live to serve."

"That's probably what makes you such a great restaurateur," she said as they walked down the hall. "You do have a knack for meeting people's needs." Whether that need was a table with a view or multiple orgasms.

"I'm going to tell you a humbling secret," he said. "Even an average man can look great when he surrounds himself with the right people. Piri has excellent chefs—minus one fantastic pastry chef, unfortunately—and a waitstaff that strives for perfection and a mixologist good enough to inspire a reboot of that '80s movie, *Cocktail.* Meanwhile, because I'm the majority owner of the place, I get the credit. Maybe my only talent is spotting talent in others."

"And nurturing it," she said, following him into the elevator. "Don't overlook the importance of that part."

Chefs were often creative, temperamental people, and Heath gave everyone in the restaurant clear, calm direction. She'd seen him shuffle employees to positions that were better suited for their personalities and bolster a hysterical waitress on a night when she'd gotten three orders wrong and dropped a tray of drinks. Without Heath's guiding influence, Cam might have chased half a dozen whims that set his career back. It struck her as sadly ironic that a man so skilled at surrounding himself with the right people in his professional life hadn't had more success at finding the right woman in his personal life.

Then again, he'd made it clear he wasn't really looking. He'd said point-blank that he was "shit at relationships." She had no reason not to believe him, but it was hard to imagine him failing at anything.

They exited the door behind the elevator banks, taking the tree-lined stone path past a garden of asters, spiky ferns and delicate white flowers that looked like miniature starbursts. Inside the gated pool area, there were two levels of chairs surrounding the long, rectangular pool—an upper deck of padded lounge chairs in the shade and another row of chairs down in the sun. Cam was stretched out in a chaise on the lower level, his face raised to the sky.

Eyes widening, he sat up when he saw Phoebe. "Need any help with sunblock?" he volunteered. "I remember how sensitive your skin is."

She laughed, wondering if all men used variations

of that line. "Goodness, everyone seems so concerned today with my skin-care regimen."

Heath hadn't looked amused by Cam's offer, but after a second, his lips twitched in a half smile. "Guess we're just very conscientious. Maybe we'll do some kind of community-awareness thing this summer—show us your tube of sunblock, get a free appetizer."

Nodding, Cam flashed Phoebe a smile. "We haven't even started brainstorming yet, and you're already inspiring us. What would we do without you?"

We'll find out soon enough, won't we? Once they got back to Atlanta, who knew when or how often she'd see either of them?

For the first time since Cam had broken up with her, she was truly glad she no longer worked at Piri. As she'd told Cam at the airport, she was a professional and he should have trusted her to behave like one after they separated. Yet she was glad her professionalism wouldn't be tested. The idea of having to face both men on a daily basis after this trip was untenable. Being around Cam could be confusing; now that her anger had faded, lots of good memories were returning. If she saw him on a regular basis, there was a chance he might eventually win her back and she knew now she didn't want that. And the idea of working with Heath every day was even worse, maintaining a platonic relationship and trying to pretend like none of this had happened...

She eyed the small outdoor bar on the other side of the gate. "I think I need a drink."

"First round's on me." Cam shot to his feet, all helpful eagerness. "Want them to swirl together a strawberry daiquiri and a piña colada? I know that's your favorite vacation drink."

He was right. Although Phoebe normally favored glasses of wine or the occasional strong martini, nothing said *vacation* like something sweet with a paper umbrella in it.

"Sure, thanks." A frozen drink would be perfect for a hot Florida afternoon.

Heath was just putting in his order when Cam pulled his phone from his pocket, his face lighting up when he saw who the caller was. "I have to take this!"

"I'll go get the drinks, then," Heath said. "The second round can be on you."

Cam barely paused to nod before hurrying off to a far corner to conduct his conversation. Phoebe sat on the edge of the pool, dipping her toes in the water. She was surprised more people weren't present, taking advantage of the gorgeous day. The only other guests in sight were a couple of college kids splashing each other in the deep end and a woman reading a book on the upper deck. Other tourists were probably at the beach; in Phoebe's opinion, there was something to be said for the lack of jellyfish in hotel pools.

Some boldly adventurous woman you are.

"Pheebs!" Cam bounded up to her, grinning from ear to ear. "You won't believe who was on the phone—the head of the tenant committee for the Regent High-Rise."

She stood. "As in, some of the most hard-to-get

condos in Buckhead? *That* high-rise?" He'd been on a waiting list for over a year.

He hugged her to him, spinning her around so that her feet actually came off the ground for a second. "I'm in! Can you believe it?"

She returned the hug, genuinely happy for him. "This is your dream! And it's way better for you than the quixotic food-truck thing."

"My God, the kitchens in those condos... The refrigerator is more like a four-hundred-pound work of art than an appliance. And there's the built-in wine fridge and the top-of-the-line ovens."

"Weird," she teased, "that some misguided people would be more excited about the stunning view and the club membership that comes with the condo than, say, the microwave model."

"Well, you know me." He laughed, but then his expression turned wistful. "You *do* know me. Phoebe, I—"

"Am I interrupting something?" Heath asked. His voice was velvet soft, yet it made Phoebe jump.

"Drinks!" She stepped forward to seize hers. "Just in time to toast Cam's news. He's going to be the newest tenant in the prestigious Regent High-Rise."

Heath looked suitably impressed. "I expect you'll have everyone over for a housewarming party that includes very expensive booze."

"Done," Cam said. "Of course, I may need to talk to my business partner about negotiating a raise..."

"Good luck with that," Heath said, his expression one of faux sympathy. "I hear he's a real hard-ass."

"Hmm." Cam took a sip of his drink. "*I* hear he's a real player who can't commit to a woman."

Phoebe sucked in a breath, surprised he'd gone there.

But Heath was unfazed, shrugging calmly. "No reason he can't be both."

HEATH NODDED ABSENTLY at whatever Cam had just said about the proposed menu, but he couldn't keep his attention on the conversation. Honestly, for all Heath knew, his business partner could have typed "grilled shoelaces with a pulverized limestone crust" into his tablet. It was difficult to focus with the angry buzzing in his ears. Heath wanted to ditch this brainstorming session and work out some aggression in the hotel gym.

How many sets of weights would it take to erase the image of Cam about to kiss Phoebe by the pool? At the sight of Cam's arms around her, Heath had been seized by a violent impulse to tackle the man.

But, intellectually, could Heath even blame him for what he was attempting? Cam had warned that he wanted her back, and his strategy was solid. He wasn't pushing too hard, but he paid her light compliments and kept peppering the conversation with intimate references. Like his smarmy "I know that's your favorite vacation drink."

Big deal. Did he think he deserved a gold star for that little nugget of trivia? Maybe he should have taken her on more vacations instead of taking her for granted.

Still… Phoebe had loved him once. Had Cam learned his lesson? If she took him back, would he treat her better, make her happy? The thought of them together made Heath want to gnash his teeth. He momentarily pondered buying Cam a food truck just to get rid of his ass. But Phoebe's romantic decisions were none of his business. He knew better than anyone that sex with another person didn't establish a claim.

Some primitive, caveman part of him wanted to forbid her to reunite with Cam—which was, of course, bullshit. She'd either laugh at Heath outright or justifiably smack him upside the head with one of her cake pans. Furthermore, if there was a chance that she and Cam could build something lasting, what right did Heath have to root against them? It wasn't as if *he* was offering her anything real.

"Yes, but you don't want to be cliché about it," Phoebe was saying now. "Right, Heath?"

He blinked at her. "Sorry, my mind was elsewhere for a minute." Or, the past forty-five of them.

She backtracked and filled him in. "Well, I get that the place is Hot and sexy is part of your theme, but that doesn't mean all the food needs to be phallic-shaped or that you have to go with obvious rumored aphrodisiacs like oysters. You want to be evocative, but not tacky."

"We need more subtle aphrodisiacs," he agreed, his mood momentarily lifting. "Like pomegranates."

Phoebe caught his eye, her lips tilting in an almost

shy, lopsided smile. As if the temptress who'd blown his mind on the balcony last night could be shy.

"Oh! There's a scallop-and-pomegranate recipe I've been experimenting with." Cam keyed some words into his tablet, seemingly oblivious to the undercurrents around him. "Thanks, Phoebe."

Her gaze left Heath's, almost reluctantly, and she nodded to her ex. "Glad I could help."

Cam set the tablet aside, his expression earnest. "Heath and I are lucky that you were able to take the time off to come to Miami. I know you've been busting your ass to get your own business off the ground, and you put that on hold."

Heath experienced a sharp pinch of shame. When he'd high-handedly bought Phoebe's airplane ticket to Miami, deciding it was easier to seek forgiveness than permission, he hadn't spared enough consideration for the fact that he and Cam weren't the only ones trying to take their careers to the next level.

Phoebe was smiling at her ex-boyfriend. "Don't make me sound like such a saint—in return for my consulting, I got a free vacation."

"Well, I'm sure I speak for both of us when I say you were a tremendous help today." He glanced around at the pool area, which was empty except for the three of them. Most hotel guests were probably inside ordering dinner or waiting for a table. "The day doesn't have to be over yet. I think we've earned some fun. What do you say to a night on the town?" His smile lingered on Phoebe long enough to make Heath's jaw clench before he turned to belatedly include Heath in the invitation, too. "Are you guys up for hitting a club?"

I'd rather hit you. "No." The refusal was automatic and curt. As soon as the word left Heath's mouth, he realized he had no right to answer for Phoebe. He tried to backpedal. "I mean, I thought I'd crash early. Before the, um, baseball game tomorrow."

"The baseball game that doesn't start until five?" Phoebe asked with a bemused smile.

"What are you, fifty?" Cam scoffed as he stood.

Heath made himself meet Phoebe's eyes, trying to look sincere. "If you want to go without me…" *Please, please don't.*

She was quiet for a long enough moment to make him nervous, then she shook her head. "We've been sitting by this gorgeous pool all afternoon without actually enjoying it. I think I'm going to swim a few laps, shower and maybe order something decadent from room service. But, Cam, you should go to some clubs. You're a great dancer," she said, lessening the sting of her refusal. "I wouldn't want Miami to miss out on your moves."

He smiled reflexively, but shot Heath a hard look. "I guess I'll catch up with the two of you tomorrow."

"Or the next day," Heath said, feeling a tightness in his chest ease. "After all, we've got the ballgame and that sous chef invited you to go on the South Beach food tour."

"Well, if nothing else, I know I'll see plenty of you on Wednesday." They had the cab ride and all that time at the airport gate. Did Cam somehow think he had a shot of rekindling his romance with her by the time passengers started boarding? "Until then." He leaned down and kissed Phoebe on the top of the head.

It was a quick peck, with nothing sexual or disrespectful about it. Yet Heath had never wanted to shove someone into a pool so badly. His hands balled into fists that didn't relax until Cam had left the pool area and the wrought iron gate swung shut behind him.

Phoebe was digging through her tote bag. Once she'd found an elastic band, she pulled her hair back into a ponytail and stood. "Getting in the pool with me?"

"Absolutely." He had to chuckle when she went down the steps and inched her way into the water by slow degrees. In contrast, he went to the deep end and cannonballed. When he came up for air, shaking water from his head like a German shepherd, she still hadn't made it in up to her shoulders. "I don't mean to rush you, but how long does this submersion process of yours take?" he called. "You do realize we have tickets to a baseball game tomorrow? I'd like to get there in time for pitching practice."

"Har har." She rolled her eyes—a gesture he sensed more than saw with the distance between them. "So I don't dive in blindly. My way works, too, hotshot. It just requires patience."

"Are patience and wimpiness the same thing?" he said, goading her.

Her hands went to her hips. "Speaking on behalf

of womankind, it might be appreciated if you men learned how to take your time more."

He stalked through the water toward her. "Was that a complaint, Mars? Or a challenge? Because I assure you, I can go very slowly if that's what you want."

"You know it wasn't a complaint." Her voice had turned husky. "These past couple of nights have been…" She seemed to give herself a mental shake. "Maybe you're right, and I should just get this over with." Then she disappeared under the water.

She surfaced about a yard away from him. "Tell me the truth—" She scrunched up her nose and muttered something under her breath before asking, "Did you say no to Cam's invitation because you know I'm more of a homebody than a party girl?"

"What? I said no because I didn't want to share you with a hundred glamorous strangers." Or with Cam. "I wanted you all to myself. What was that you were mumbling about truth?"

"Oh." She kicked her legs out in front of her, scissoring past him at a lazy speed. "I just think it's a tad hypocritical for me to demand the truth when part of my reason for this trip sprang from trying to deceive someone."

Heath stilled. Yes, he'd thrown out making her ex jealous as an initial excuse for spending time together, but deception had nothing to do with what was between them now. There'd been nothing false about how she'd responded to him last night, about the bliss of losing himself inside her and watching her back arch as an orgasm shuddered through her. Every kiss they'd shared had been its own truth. *Jesus—you're not actually going to* say *that, are you?* What was happening to him?

Instead, he joked, "I was never much of a truth guy. I preferred dare."

"Truth or dare—man, Gwen used to cause more trouble at slumber parties with that game."

"I can imagine."

"I haven't played in years." She pulled herself onto a bench built into the wall of the pool. "Truth or dare, Heath?"

"Dare."

She nodded crisply, her long ponytail stirring the water. "I dare you to tell the truth—"

"You cheated." Devious vixen.

"Have you ever been in love?"

The question startled him. She'd known him for years. Why probe at his romantic past now? Did it have anything to do with her spending all day with a former love?

"Yes," he admitted. "I have been in love, believe it or not. I was a sophomore in college, and I met her in November. I fell so hard that even though we'd only been dating a few weeks, I invited her to spend Thanksgiving with my family. Where she met my stepbrother." He scowled.

His feelings for Tara had long ago faded into dusty memory, but it still stung that his erstwhile champion had been the one to betray him. "Victor is two years older than me, and was thrilled when our parents got married. He could have been a dick about it, annoyed to suddenly have a little brother in the house, sharing his wealth and privilege, but he treated me well from day one. And he influenced others to do the same." Vic had stared down those who called Heath "chunk." Or the even more vicious "lard-ass."

It was under Victor's guidance that Heath had developed his self-esteem, not letting others' opinions define him. Then when his growth spurt had hit and his outward appearance caught up to his confidence, his popularity had exploded—especially when he went away to college, where no one had memories or awkward photos of the kid he'd been before.

His freshman year of university had been a very good year.

He tried to focus on those memories and not the anguish of standing up as Victor's best man. "I didn't know it at the time, but Victor kissed my girlfriend while we were there at Thanksgiving. They swore to each other it would never happen again, but then I made the mistake of bringing her home for Christmas." His mouth twisted. "They were engaged a year and a half later. She's currently expecting twins."

"Oh, Heath."

He gave a shrug of manly nonchalance. "It doesn't bother me anymore."

"Still, I'm so sorry. Sorry for what they did and sorry I pried." She pushed off the wall and swam toward him. "Did you start your no-relationship policy after they got together?"

"No, I went out and found myself another girlfriend, determined to be happy and wildly in love.

It wasn't until I brought her home for the first time, eager to show off how successfully I'd recovered, that she and I both realized I wasn't over Tara. My girl-friend felt understandably betrayed, and the breakup was messy. After that came a string of casual affairs. I had one pretty serious girlfriend while I was getting ready to open Piri. There were days I worked ten or twelve hours—you know how it is—and she felt ne-glected. When she left in tears, I decided that maybe I'd be better off just sticking to the affairs, easy ar-rangements where no one was hurt by unfulfilled expectations."

He knew how some people saw him. A particularly angry ex had once used the word *womanizer,* which he resented. "I don't date as some kind of payback for a broken heart. I just don't see how it would be fair to a woman to drag out a relationship with no future."

"But if you found someone you thought you could have a future with?" Phoebe asked softly.

"Hasn't happened yet." *Really?* Or had he met a woman he could imagine falling for…except that she was with someone else at the time?

Phoebe wound her arms around his neck. "I'm sure your stepbrother has many fine qualities," she said in a skeptical tone that belied her words, "but your girlfriend was a fool to give you up."

"Very true. But if she'd had better taste in men, we might not be here now, and I wouldn't get to appreci-ate how lovely you look in the moonlight." He lowered his head slowly, kissing her with teasing gentleness. She sighed into his mouth, her tongue meeting his in the same slow, unhurried rhythm she'd used to glide through the water.

But then she wrapped her legs around his waist. His hands dropped to her hips and he cradled her closer against him, his kisses growing hungrier.

When he raised his head, he could hear his own ragged breathing. "Truth or dare, Phoebe?"

"Truth," she said promptly.

As expected. "Tell me the truth—are you brave enough to hand me your bikini top?"

Pulling away, she gave him a glare of mock outrage. "That sounds like a dare in disguise."

"Oh, were we playing by the rules?" he asked silkily. "I thought, given the way *you* cheated…"

She dragged her hand through the water, then scooped her arm up to splash him.

Laughing, he wiped droplets from his eyes. "I take it that's your ungracious way of saying no, you aren't brave enough?"

She pursed her lips, her expression turning stubborn. When she turned her head to study the surrounding pool area, as if she might actually remove her top, lust roared through him. There was no one else here, and they didn't hear anyone on the path beyond. He held his breath, the only sound the evening breeze rustling through the palm trees.

Almost as if in slow motion, she reached her arms behind her back, untying the knot between her shoulder blades. The pale material floated in front of her breasts, bobbing on the water but still covering her. Then she crossed her arms behind her neck. When she dropped them again, the bikini top drifted away from her. Her body was creamy perfection, the moonlight glistening on her wet breasts, and her nipples were tight, puckered buds he couldn't wait to lick and suck again.

He took one step toward her, and she gave him a coy smile.

"I think I've had enough of the pool for tonight," she said, inching backward.

He considered persuading her to stay, but there were so many more things he could do to her in the room, without risk of being caught and thrown off hotel property. So he remained where he was, enjoying the view. Her breasts bounced gently as she climbed the steps, each sway and jiggle going straight to his dick.

Giving him a saucy smile, she stepped into her sandals and wrapped a large beach towel around herself, tucking it in so securely it was practically a terry-cloth evening gown—strapless with a provocative slit at the leg worthy of the red carpet. She reached beneath the towel and gave a little wiggle as she shifted from one foot to the other. Then there was a splash next to him, temporarily jolting him from his mesmerized stare. It took him a second to realize the bottom half of her bikini had just landed next to him in the water.

Phoebe gave him a finger wave and sauntered toward the gate, leaving Heath with a raging hard-on and the certainty that nothing the Miami club scene offered could top the evening he was about to have.

I CAN'T BELIEVE I just did that. Phoebe almost giggled aloud at her own audacity, but she didn't want to draw any extra attention to herself as she pressed the button for the elevator. As long as the towel stayed in place, she wasn't actually exposing herself to anyone, but just the same, she'd prefer that other guests in the lobby went about their own business and didn't look too closely.

Although she'd sure as hell enjoyed Heath's gaze on her.

His expression of stunned reverence when her bikini top had floated away had been priceless. It was obvious he'd only been teasing her with his dare and hadn't really expected her to do it. But untying those strings had been the least she could do after the way he'd opened up to her. For all that he was one of her best friends, he rarely discussed past relationships. *Guess now I know why.* It couldn't be easy, spending time with his family and having to face his brother with someone Heath had once loved.

The elevator doors opened with a ding that almost made her jump, and she darted inside. But just as she was expelling a breath of relief that she had the elevator to herself, Heath appeared, his eyes glittering.

He gave her a smile that was either pure worship or dire warning.

She gulped.

"Quite a show you put on," he said as the doors closed. "What's your plan for an encore?"

Oh, boy. "I think I remember most of a tap-dance routine from middle school."

His grin widened and he stepped closer, advancing until he'd backed her into the corner of the elevator. Her skin prickled with awareness, her senses awash in Heath—the jagged sound of his labored breathing, the warm, masculine musk of him after hours in the sun, the sleekness of his still-damp skin and corded muscle.

"I was thinking less tap and more nudity," he murmured. "The only thing that's keeping me from reaching for that towel is knowing there could be cameras in the elevator. Or would you like that, Phoebe? Being exposed to admiring eyes? Letting them enjoy the curve of your breasts, your firm, round ass, your creamy thighs?"

In reality, she didn't want any such thing, but the words and the make-believe were thrilling. Even more thrilling? The way Heath was devouring her with his eyes, as if he'd never wanted anything more than he craved her. She loved that look, could get more addicted to it than she was to her morning coffee or dark chocolate.

The elevator chimed, letting them know they'd reached their floor. Heath pulled the key card from the pocket of his trunks and held it up with a smirk. "If you want me to let you into the room, you have to do what I say." His deep, authoritative voice was more potent than any supposed aphrodisiac.

Her heart kicked into triple time, and she wanted him so much she almost launched herself into his arms then and there. *Cameras, Pheeb, cameras.* The mental warning didn't lessen her ardor as much as it should have. "What do you want me to do?" she asked, her whispered voice thick with need.

"I want to watch you."

That night in his loft came back to her, the words she'd confessed to him. *I imagined him catching me naked. Imagined what it would be like for him to watch me touch myself.* Heath was giving her the fantasy. She nodded, too turned on to articulate words.

They silently exited the elevator in unison. Part of her wanted to rush down the hall, but aching arousal left her too unsteady on her feet. Besides, it felt sexier to make him wait—make them both wait—and delay their mutual pleasure for these last few charged minutes. It wasn't only being chilly from the pool that had her shivering as he opened the door.

"Wait." He held out a hand, stopping her just inside the entryway. He went to the bed and turned on the wall-mounted reading light that shone down on the mattress. Leaving the rest of the suite in darkness, he stepped back, blending into the shadows.

A spotlight. Nerves somersaulted in the pit of her stomach, and her throat felt dry. She wavered for a split second. Was she the kind of girl who could do this?

Damn right you are. She was the kind of woman who could seize her own pleasure without guilt or apology. And in the meantime, she'd give Heath a night he'd never forgot. Affairs didn't last forever, but the memories could. She strode toward the bed in its circle of muted light and let her towel fall to the floor.

As she reached the edge of the mattress, she

stopped, cupping her breasts. They were so full, so heavy with sensation. She rubbed her thumbs over the taut peaks, letting her eyes close as her head fell back. After a moment, she stretched forward, giving Heath an eyeful of "firm, round ass" as she crawled onto the center of the bed. When she heard him hiss in a breath, she smiled over her shoulder, unable to make out more than his broad silhouette in the dark corner of the room.

"I could be anyone," he told her, his voice so strained it was almost unrecognizable. "Does that excite you?"

She didn't answer, merely rolled onto her back, feet pointed toward him. Maybe later she'd tell him. The fantasy of a stranger, as hot as it was, couldn't hold a candle to the reality of Heath as a lover. The things he'd done to her... She was surprised to find herself getting even more turned on. She'd been wet and swollen since walking into the room, so how did the memory of Heath's hands on her make her even *more* horny? Wasn't there a limit? *Not with him.*

She curled her fingers around her inner thigh, sliding her leg to the side, knowing she was on full display before him. Her other hand she trailed from between her breasts down her abdomen, stopping to swirl a slow circle around her navel before passing over the springy curls in the neatly trimmed V between her legs. Heath groaned, and she felt the vibration of it rumble through her. Instead of going directly for her clitoris, she skated her fingers over the velvety folds, her skin dewy with her own juices.

On impulse, she raised one finger to her lips, tasting the earthy flavor.

Heath tensed, and his body jerked forward. She thought he was about to join her on the bed.

While she would have welcomed him inside her, she was glad when he remained where he was, giving them this decadent experience. Her hand returned to her core, and this time she pushed her middle finger against the engorged bud. Fleeting shyness gripped her. Heath had seen her naked repeatedly—had undressed her himself and filled her deeply. How was it possible that this felt more intimate, more vulnerable, than sex?

"Phoebe." His voice had a raw, broken quality to it that sent her into motion.

She rubbed in an urgent rhythm, throwing her other arm across her closed eyes. This wasn't about gauging his reaction or worrying about how she looked in an abandoned moment. This was about the escalating need pounding through her and chasing the hovering climax that promised to reduce her to ruin. She twisted her hips, writhing against her own hand as tremors started deep within her. Still stroking her clit, she lowered her other hand so that she could penetrate herself with two fingers.

Heath made a low, guttural sound that joined her muffled cries as the cresting waves of pleasure broke, swamping her with brutal ecstasy and carrying her out beyond a place of coherent thought or reason. She heard herself make a noise like a sob, but there was a smile on her face.

"Fuck, that was hot." Heath's voice was awestruck. And closer than she'd expected. She hadn't realized he'd moved, had lost track of time in the throes of orgasm.

She smiled drowsily, enjoying the lassitude seeping through her veins but hoping her energy recovered quickly. From the expression on his face, they weren't done yet. "Enough of an encore for you?"

He shoved down the swim trunks he still wore, his erection massive. "You got a standing ovation."

She held her arms out, encouraging him to join her. "I think it's time for some audience participation, don't you?"

He put on a condom with record speed, then stretched over her.

Propped up on her elbows, she met him halfway for a hungry kiss that highlighted exactly how much he wanted her. Had she ever felt this desirable before?

He fisted a hand in her hair, tugging gently until she drew her head back, meeting his eyes. "You make me crazy." His hoarse, admiring tone made it clear the words were a compliment.

She batted her eyelashes, her smile sly. "Who, me?" It might go to her head, having so much power over a man like Heath, except that he wielded the same control over her. How would she ever get enough of him?

The past few days had taught her that Heath was skilled at foreplay, but right now he was a man driven to the brink, his expression almost harsh as he nudged her thighs farther apart and surged into her with one forceful thrust. Her breath caught, but she was slick from her earlier climax, and there was no discomfort, only spiraling need. Locking her legs around his waist, she arched up to meet him, closing her eyes at the sheer bliss of having him inside her.

"Phoebe." His voice was low, commanding, as he brushed his knuckles over her cheek. "Look at me."

The request surprised her, but she opened her eyes, dazed by his possessive expression as he stared down at her. By how he made her burn for him. By the almost unbearably intense connection between them. Gazes locked, he laced his fingers through hers, holding her hands next to her head as he pistoned into her, pressing against her still-sensitive clit with every shove of his hips. Her orgasm came faster than expected, wringing his name from her in a sharp cry. Unable to keep her eyes open any longer, she squeezed them shut and tightened her hold on him as he came, wanting him, in that moment, to be part of her.

Earlier, when he'd watched her from the shadows, he'd teased, "I could be anyone." Nothing was further from the truth. No one but Heath had ever made her feel this way. And it was impossible to imagine anyone else ever would.

11

As the shuttle bus to the stadium rolled to a stop, Phoebe grinned broadly, as eager as a kid on Christmas morning.

Heath regarded her with amusement. "You're downright giddy."

"I love baseball games," she said, descending the steps onto the pavement. "You know that."

"True." He pulled sunglasses from his pocket and slid them on. "But do you know how damaging it will be to my ego if today's game turns out to be your favorite part of the vacation?"

She grinned. "Your ego is sizable enough to take the hit."

He swatted her on the ass in playful retribution for the taunt, and heat shimmied through her, momentarily eclipsing her excitement for the game. But then they entered the stadium, and she breathed in the scents of popcorn and beer, the same smells that had greeted her when her uncle had taken her to her first game at age seven. This ballpark was a little smaller than what she was used to in Atlanta, and the club had—mercifully—opted to close the retractable roof in deference to the day's heat index. The stadium seating was a sea of blue, and Heath led her to their spots near the visitors' dugout.

As Phoebe understood it, when the grandparents she'd never met discovered their seventeen-year-old daughter was pregnant, they'd disowned her, forbidding their son, Mike, to have contact with his older sister. But once he was an adult, he'd tracked her down. A high school gym coach with summers off, his visits had usually fallen smack in the middle of the baseball season. Since Phoebe's mother disliked the heat, the ticket prices and the lengthy drive, she'd often sent Phoebe and Mike alone. Those ballgames had been some of the most enjoyable memories of her childhood—an escape from the severe environment of her house to a place where you were actually *encouraged* to yell and holler and your favorite uncle bought you all the sodas you wanted, caffeine be damned.

She was so happy to be back in a stadium, absorbing the energy of a small but enthusiastic crowd, that she didn't even mind that her team was having an off game. After the first pitch, Heath declared that they were going to celebrate each time the team scored with a kiss, but by the fifth inning, that had only happened twice. Meanwhile, sitting shoulder to shoulder with Heath, she was getting a whole new appreciation for how dirty baseball could sound, what with all the talk of bases and scoring and mounds and getting wood.

The fifth inning wasn't looking very promising, with only one out left with their team up to bat, but at least Phoebe had her soft pretzel to make her happy. She bit off a corner, then noticed Heath's incredulous look. Was he surprised by how much she was putting away? She'd finished a hot dog and nachos earlier and had stated her intention to get popcorn before the seventh-inning stretch. Her appetite had been off the charts for the past couple of days. Marathon sex made a girl *hungry*.

But it turned out Heath wasn't judging the quantity of food, just her selections. "Didn't you notice the regional snack options here?" he demanded. "Conch fritters, ceviche, malanga chips."

She washed down her pretzel with a sip of cold beer. "All yummy choices, but I don't come to a baseball game to eat ceviche. Where's your ballpark spirit?"

"Being held hostage in a dark basement by my taste buds. Considering how refined your palate is, I can't believe you love generic stadium food so much."

"Food snob."

"Hell, yes. That's why I went into the restaurant business—plus, years of experience trying to charm more popular kids into liking me makes me suited to the hospitality industry. But mostly, I work to advance culinary excellence because my stepfather's housekeeper spoiled me silly. Fresh produce, unique ingredients, amazing yet unpretentious skill. Then I got to college and realized what other kids my age were eating." He shuddered at the memory. "I was immediately convinced there was some conspiracy to kill the country's best and brightest through dorm food."

She laughed at his outraged expression. "So even as a teenager you identified yourself as one of our nation's 'best and brightest'?"

"False modesty benefits no one, Mars."

She laughed again, but then the crack of the bat drew her attention to the field. One of the Braves hit a home run, and both Phoebe and Heath leaped to their feet, cheering—which earned a few disgruntled glances from the home-team fans surrounding them. Heath framed her face in his hands and stole a quick kiss.

He leaned back with a grin. "I'm usually more of a fine wine and aged bourbon kind of guy, but you make domestic beer taste good."

They regained their seats, watching as the next hitter jogged up to home plate. If the Braves scored again, it would be a tie ballgame.

A few minutes later, Heath asked, "So you know my story—what about yours? How'd you get into food and beverage?"

Suddenly, she could smell vanilla and hear faint humming. Something bittersweet twitched in the vicinity of her heart. "In all the time Cam and I were together, he never me asked that. I think cooking is so much an integral part of his personality that he just assumes other people are like him."

"Is that your way of evading the question?" Heath

asked. He was a man who respected privacy, and she knew he wouldn't push if she was uncomfortable.

She could change the subject, comment on the runner who'd just made it to second, but hell, she was twenty-five years old. At some point she should be able to share bits of her past without them getting stuck in her throat. Otherwise, her upbringing was wielding way too much power over her, keeping her from becoming more.

"I told you that my mother didn't mean to have me. I just…happened." She ducked her gaze, wondering if she'd ever get past this lingering shame, as if her birth was somehow her fault.

Heath squeezed her hand, and she was so grateful for his unspoken support that she wanted to kiss him. A for-real kiss, not the playful pecks they'd been exchanging in the name of baseball. But if she started that, she'd never get through this explanation. Making out with Heath was infinitely more fun than dwelling on her childhood.

"To my mom's credit," Phoebe said, "even though she hadn't planned for me, she took care of me. We just never had a warm relationship. I don't remember hugs or bedtime stories. But I remember birthday cakes." Every February 18 without fail. "God knows why she honored that tradition so fervently, but every year, she created some baked treat even more delicious than the year before. She baked at Christmas, too, and I think waking up to the scent of zucchini bread in the oven, or chocolate cakes cooling on the baker's rack, was the closest I came to feeling loved.

When I realized that I could do that for a living, that I could provide people with some measure of joy… Suffice to say, it was the only career I ever considered."

He studied her for a long, silent moment. Then he shook his head, his smile self-deprecating. "So to sum up, *you* chose a vocation because you wanted to spread love and joy, while I picked mine motivated by a selfish desire for better dining options. Yeah, that sounds about right."

Even though she knew he was joking, his words left her discomfited. Did he not see himself as someone who had love to offer? She found that sad. From the story he'd told her yesterday, he'd only truly been in love once—and it hadn't ended well. While she believed he was over the woman, it couldn't be easy to move past betrayal when it married into the family.

Still, she hated to think that he would sentence himself to being alone forever rather than try again. She almost pushed the issue, but worried he might think she was hinting at some kind of emotional commitment from him. That had never been on the table. Hell, just yesterday he'd acted as if he didn't care whether she stayed with him for the night or went clubbing with her ex-boyfriend. As glad as she was that she'd remained with Heath, and as wonderful a night as they'd shared, her eyes were wide-open. A vacation fling did not a lasting relationship make.

Besides, baseball games were no more about an angsty analyzation of feelings than they were ceviche. So she returned her attention to the field. The Braves came back in the final innings, scoring four times. Heath kissed her for each of them, and her escalating physical response began to edge out her earlier unease.

As they stood to leave, she noticed an elderly couple a few rows behind them, affectionately bickering about the best route to get home. The woman, who was probably in her late sixties, was calling the man an old fool, and he retorted that she was a know-it-all even as he helped her to her feet and she patted his arm. Phoebe grinned inwardly, almost able to imagine a sixty-year-old Heath chastising her for her lousy taste in stadium food while she chowed down on cheese fries and funnel cake.

Heath followed her gaze. "What's so fun— Uh-oh. Ma'am? Be right back," he told Phoebe. He sprinted up the rows to retrieve the purse that the elderly woman had left behind, then chased after her.

Phoebe thought it was silly to make him backtrack after delivering it, so she simply caught up to where he was now chatting with the older couple. Whatever he'd just said made them laugh, and seeing their faces warmed Phoebe. Heath spread joy, too. He just seemed reluctant to create any for himself.

IT WAS ON the shuttle ride back to the hotel that the truth caught up to Phoebe. Maybe there'd been a time not too long ago when she'd imagined a future with Cam, but now, when she pictured the years ahead, it was all too easy to picture Heath by her side. Watching that elderly couple at the park had made her wistful for what they shared. There were two people who hadn't been afraid to build a future.

I've screwed up. Badly. She couldn't quite call sleeping with Heath a mistake—it was hard to regret the best sex of her life—but she could no longer deny that she was falling for him.

How many other women had made that error over the years? During the time she'd worked for Heath, she'd witnessed several girlfriends get their hopes up—females of varying backgrounds, careers, ages and races. Entirely different women, same end result.

She could barely look at him as they rode the elevator up to their floor. Just the sight of his profile made her want to kiss him, which in turn made her miserable. By this time tomorrow, he'd be officially off limits to her. So she kept her eyes straight ahead, but he met her gaze in the mirrored doors.

With a smile, he reached over to tug on her ball cap. "You are so cute."

Right. Cute. No trace of va, va *or* voom at the moment. And yet, sitting in that hard plastic chair scarfing down junk food, she'd felt more like herself than she had in days. *This is the real me.* Why did it have to be the real her who'd stupidly fallen for him, instead of the vacation persona she could shed as soon as she stepped on the plane?

When they entered the hotel room, he reached for her hand, stepping forward to kiss her. It was practically a conditioned response—most of the time they'd spent in this suite, they'd been all over each other. An answering desire swirled in her, but she ducked away at the last minute, swallowing a lump of emotion and trying to figure out an explanation for her lackluster mood. She'd had a lot of fun at the game and it wasn't as if Heath had done anything wrong. He'd been completely honest with her, never misrepresenting himself. *I'm a selfish hedonist. I don't have relationships.*

"What's wrong?" he asked, the concern in his tone only making her want to cry more.

"To be honest…" No, honesty was not what the moment required. Telling him that she was teetering on the brink of falling in love might well destroy their friendship. He'd avoid her once they returned to Atlanta, and the thought of him no longer being in her life… "I'm not feeling very well." A partial truth anyway.

He clucked his tongue sympathetically. "I warned you about all that stadium food."

She wasn't suffering from heartburn; this was impending heartache.

"Can I get you anything?"

"No. I just want to take a quick shower, pack up my stuff and get to bed."

"Okay." He gave her space, not even trying to talk his way into her shower, which was a first.

Afterward, while she was folding clothes that felt like a stranger's, Heath handed her a square of material, "Don't forget this."

His T-shirt? *Oh, God, Phoebe, no crying.* Sexy, sophisticated seductresses didn't blubber when it was time to bid a lover a fond farewell. She swallowed.

"Thank you." She should give it back, yet she tucked it with her things.

While he took his own shower, she crawled into bed, wondering what would happen when he joined her. Would he want to make love? Could she lose herself in that physical connection one last time without having an emotional breakdown? She knew she could play the "I have a headache" card and he would respect that, but then she'd also be shortchanging herself a final opportunity to be with him.

She was still debating what she wanted when he padded into the room. The mattress dipped beneath his weight, and he slid an arm across her, hauling her against him.

"Don't worry," he murmured, removing the burden of a decision, "I'm not making a move. I just want to be close."

The tears she refused to shed pricked even more viciously. Heath Jensen, unrepentant ladies' man, wanted to cuddle? In some ways, this was worse than if they'd had sex. Because snuggling against him as he stroked her hair made it too tempting to believe this was something real. Something more than reclaiming her sensuality through a vacation fling and fantasy fulfillment.

"Sorry you aren't feeling good," he said. "At least you'll be home soon. As nice as it is to get away, it's always a relief to sleep in your own bed again."

A relief? Right now, sleeping in her own bed sounded like the loneliest outcome imaginable. She squeezed her eyes shut and focused on keeping her breathing even.

Her experience with men was that he'd probably be asleep in moments—they seldom seemed to have as much trouble shutting down their brains to relax—but it was at least fifteen minutes later when he whispered, "You awake, Mars?"

"Uh-huh."

"I was just thinking. This…you and me?"

Her heart raced, and she held her breath.

"We enjoy sex with each other," he said with his typical bluntness. "I know we set tomorrow as our expiration date, but that's not set in stone. There's no reason we couldn't occasionally do this again. Back in Atlanta, I mean."

Dashed hope was a very specific and cruel pain. How had she let herself think, even for a minute, that he was going to admit to having strong feelings for her? That he might tell her she was important enough for him to give up the no-relationships philosophy that guided his adult life? *Idiot.* Instead, he'd offered the same damn thing Cameron had when he'd dumped her—the opportunity for no-strings booty calls.

But worse than what he'd said was her response… "You're right. There's no real reason we can't." Because she wasn't sure she could make the clean break yet, knowing what she'd be missing once she gave him up.

Heath let out a small sigh of contentment, kissed her temple and fell asleep minutes later, leaving her awake and fuming, unable to decide which one of them she was angrier at.

THROUGH THE OVERHEAD SPEAKER, the captain announced that they were preparing for final descent into Atlanta. Phoebe stared forlornly out the window. Being so high in the air, unable to see the ground below, you could almost forget it was down there. But eventually, your time in the clouds came to an end and real life loomed larger and larger as it rushed up to meet you.

Next to her, Heath tucked her hair behind her ear, craning his head for a better look at her face. "Everything okay? You've been uncharacteristically quiet the entire flight."

"Have I?" she murmured, wondering at his word choice. Uncharacteristic? She'd been soft-spoken her whole life and was generally the mild yin to Gwen's boisterous yang. It was everything *before* today's flight that had been out of character—an impulsive jaunt to Miami, casual sex, stripping off her bathing suit in a public pool.

Phoebe liked that brave and brazen girl. *But I don't want to be her every day.*

At lunch on Monday, Cam had told her she'd changed. Those changes had been enough to make him want her again. And they'd worked on Heath, too—so much that he'd given their affair a stay of execution and left the door open for occasionally seeing each other again. A gambling woman might try to string together enough "occasionallys" to build a relationship, but then what?

Sure, Heath enjoyed the Phoebe who wore expensive lingerie and gave balcony blow jobs. But how long could the Phoebe who sang show tunes while frosting cakes in her yoga pants hold his interest? His short attention span in romantic entanglements was legendary. The warning she'd received at the awards luncheon rang in her ears. *You might think you're going to be different, but trust me, honey, plenty of women thought that.*

She flashed him a brief smile, hoping it looked more genuine than it felt. He'd given her a lot these past few days—experiences she wouldn't trade for anything in the world—and she didn't want him to think she regretted them. Hadn't that been his fear that first day, when he'd suggested they not have sex? "I'm being noble," he'd said. Because he hadn't wanted to hurt her when the affair inevitably ended. Time to show him she could be adult and mature about this.

"I had a lot of fun in Miami," she told him.

He waggled his eyebrows at her. "If I didn't already know your stance on airplane lavatories, I'd say we could still fit in a few more minutes of fun."

"Okay, first, ew. But, second…you shouldn't make jokes like that anymore."

"Who was joking?"

"I'm serious. A few weeks ago, I was hurting and feeling vulnerable after Cam left me and I turned to you. I wanted you to help me find out if I can be sexy—which I can—and I wanted to make Cam jealous, which we did. You promised me four nights and they were…unforgettable. But since we accomplished everything we set out to do, don't you think it's best to return to how things were?"

12

HEATH WAS SO stunned by her words that he couldn't form any of his own. The woman who had started the day snuggled against his chest was giving him the brush-off at twenty thousand feet? *Thanks, Heath—you made me feel desirable and helped me win back the attention of my ex. You're a pal.* His knee-jerk reaction was outrage, but what had he expected? After all, he'd outlined those very objectives when persuading her to come to Miami. How could he blame her for taking him up on exactly what he'd offered?

"Just to clarify." He tried not to sound like a man who'd just been skewered with his own words. "By 'how things were,' you mean…?"

"We'll be friends, of course. I hope we'll always be friends." Her earnest tone made him want to snarl. "Platonic ones. I know what you said last night, but I'm not really cut out for the whole 'benefits' arrangement."

So his going out on a limb to find out if she might

want more from him had meant nothing. He swallowed back a string of curse words, unaccustomed to being blindsided like this. *Which is why you quit having messy emotional relationships, remember?*

"Besides," Phoebe added, lowering her gaze and toying with a loose thread in the armrest, "we don't want to get in each other's way when it comes to, um, seeing other people."

Dread and disbelief roiled through him. Was she reconciling with Cam? Was that why she didn't care whether she saw Heath again? *They have history. All the two of you had was a few days of passion.*

White-hot, all-consuming, breath-stealing passion.

This was far worse than when Tara had left him for Victor because it wasn't some out-of-the-blue betrayal. No, Heath himself had damn well orchestrated this. Yet the thought of seeing her reunited with her ex, having to make small talk with them at parties and dinners, fighting not to imagine them together in private... His gut clenched, and he almost reached for an airsickness bag.

Instead, he forced his expression into one of bland amiability. He wasn't a monk, and he wasn't pathetic. If his own love life stayed busy enough, he wouldn't have time to dwell on Phoebe's. "I couldn't agree more. There are a lot of women whose calls I haven't returned for the past few weeks. They'll be glad to hear from me."

There was a little hitch in her breathing, but he suspected that was just a reaction to the plane's lowering altitude. Because she sounded perfectly calm when she said, "Exactly." Then she affectionately *patted his hand*, like he was her damn grandfather.

They hit the ground with a squeal of wheels on pavement and the thump of landing gear. Not a moment too soon. If Heath didn't get off the plane immediately, he might say something he really regretted. Like "please don't leave me."

He might not have the girl—yet again—but he still had his pride and he intended to keep it intact.

No tears, no tears, no tears. Blinking fiercely, Phoebe kept up her silent mantra as she, Heath and Cam rode the escalator leading to the exit. The plan had been for Heath to drive her home, but she had no idea how she'd survive the ride. It had taken everything she had to smile brightly at him on the plane when he'd implied that he couldn't wait to resume boinking a variety of women. Hell, if they'd had the same smitten flight attendant from their trip to Miami, he might not have even waited until they got off the plane. He could have joined that mile-high club. Assuming he wasn't already a member.

The thought left a sour taste in her mouth, which she knew was irrational. She'd been perfectly aware of Heath's history before he'd ever kissed her. Before their time in Miami. Before she'd practically begged him to have sex with her. *Oh, God.* There was no way she could handle a car ride with him right now.

As the three of them stepped off the escalator, she cleared her throat. "I was thinking…maybe I'll grab a cab. Your loft is the opposite direction from my place."

Heath swiveled to look at her. "That's ridiculous. Why would you pay for a cab ride when I said I'd take you home? That's the kind of favor one friend does for another, right?" His subtle emphasis on *friend* had Cam raising his eyebrows.

"Or I can drive her," Cam said. "It's on my way, more or less."

"Yeah," Heath agreed. "I guess she is closer to you."

She was so relieved that she flashed Cam a brilliant smile. "Thank you so much!" With that solved, she strode eagerly toward the sliding doors, wanting to put this all behind her. "Heath, I don't know when I'll see you again—heaven knows I owe James a ton of overtime—so…"

"Right." He reached over to give her a one-armed hug. It was less contact than he gave his favorite restaurant customers, but it was enough of a reminder of their physical intimacy that her eyes burned. "I'll be pretty busy, too. Take care of yourself, sweetheart."

She flinched hard at that. *So much for being one of a kind.* The tears were threatening in earnest now, so she didn't even try to squeak out a goodbye, just gave him a curt nod and escaped outside.

After a moment, Cam caught up to her—which was good, since she'd just realized she had no idea where he was parked. She didn't know where she was going, only that it needed to be away from Heath Jensen.

"We're back that way," Cam said. She'd only heard that gentle tone from him once, when she'd gotten a lousy review from a food critic over a year ago. He hadn't even sounded that sympathetic when he'd broken up with her. He waited until they were buckled into his car, then asked, "So you and Heath…?"

"There is no me and Heath. And the less said about it, the better."

"Understood." He turned the radio to her favorite station and didn't say another word until they reached her apartment. Once in the parking garage, he popped the trunk open. "I'll get your suitcase."

She was so despondent that she let him, not bothering to point out that it rolled and that she could easily get it herself. Nothing felt easy right now, not even inhaling and exhaling. Each breath was like a tiny shard caught in her lungs. At the top of the steps, she unlocked the front door and called out Gwen's name. There was no answer, and Phoebe had mixed feelings about her friend's absence. She didn't particularly feel like being alone with her miserable thoughts right now, but she wasn't ready to face the steaming platter of "I told you so" her roommate would no doubt be serving.

"Do you want a cup of coffee?" she asked Cam impulsively. "Least I could do to say thanks for the ride."

"I'd love one."

She went into the kitchen, expecting him to have a seat at the table or on the bar stool, but he trailed after her. Breathing in the clean, sharp scent of his cologne was oddly disorienting; it should be familiar, perhaps giving her a sense of nostalgia. Instead, it was like hearing a song you used to really love and realizing you no longer remembered the words. But the aroma of coffee took over the kitchen as she ground fresh beans. After she added water to the pot and turned it on, Cam stepped closer, his expression pensive.

"I don't know if I should offer my apologies that things didn't work out with you and Jensen...or if I should feel encouraged."

"Encouraged?"

He reached for her in what she assumed was going to be a consoling hug, but then he cupped her shoulders and leaned toward her. "Dare I hope that I'm what caused the rift? That Heath sensed a connection still there between you and me? I want you back, Phoebe." His eyes slid closed, and his face angled toward hers.

"Oh, *hell*, no." She shoved against his chest. "Is this why you offered to drive me home? To hit on me?"

"I offered because I care about you," he said, his expression all wounded confusion. "And I thought... Doesn't matter. Clearly, I thought wrong."

She sighed. Oh, the irony of the day's events. "Look, Cam, you know I was crazy about you, but you threw that away. You *chose* to move on. I didn't have a choice, but I moved on, too."

"By sleeping with Heath." His jaw clenched.

"Don't make me slap you. I'm a grown woman and I can sleep in whatever bed I want."

"Of course you can. Women's rights, sexual equality—I'm all for them. I didn't mean to sound angry at you. I'm mad at myself for putting you in this situation. And mad at *him*. That bastard knows you're special, but he exploited—"

"Cam, it's sweet that you're trying to be protective." Weird, but sweet. In an archaic "this is none of your business" kind of way.

He looked abashed. "Then, we're really done?"

"Really and truly."

"Oh." His smile was lopsided, tinged with regret. "Maybe I'll skip the coffee and just get going."

"Give me a few weeks to work through any 'all men are scum' feelings and maybe we can grab a cup of coffee. Or I can help you with new recipes," she offered, feeling benevolent. "We have no future together, but, damn, you can cook."

"Thank you. And, Phoebe? For what it's worth, you seemed happy in Miami. With him. I'm sorry it didn't work out."

"Yeah." Her vision blurred, and she swallowed hard. "So am I."

"HEY, NEIGHBOR."

At the cheerful female voice, Heath turned from his mailbox to find the pretty brunette he frequently ran into at the building's gym. "Jessa."

She looked at the stack of envelopes and magazines in his hands. "Someone's popular. Or you just get a crap ton of bills—God knows *I* do," she said with a laugh.

"I was out of town." He nodded toward the suitcase propped against the wall. "Just got back this afternoon."

"Then, you probably don't have much in the way of groceries. Want to grab dinner?" she asked. "We always say we should, but since our schedules never seem to match up…"

No, he didn't want to grab dinner. He wanted to go upstairs and… What? Sulk? Recall the night he'd seared scallops for Phoebe and tried to convince her of how sexy she was? What would be the point? That sexy woman was probably with Cam at this precise moment. When Cameron had volunteered to give her a ride home, she'd lit up like Fourth of July fireworks, then practically sprinted from the airport.

Heath had told her once that he wouldn't judge her, but he was having difficulty living up to that promise. Because he thought she'd made an asinine decision. Cam hadn't appreciated her, yet she'd taken him back? The chef didn't deserve her. *Oh, and you do?* What had Heath added to her life besides orgasms that any top-of-the-line vibrator could duplicate?

"Heath?" Jessa frowned, looking concerned. "Are you okay? If you're tired from traveling, never mind about the dinner invitation. I—"

"Actually, I would love to go." He and Phoebe had agreed that their lives would return to normal. Spending time with beautiful women was Heath's normal.

It just wouldn't be with the beautiful woman he wanted.

PHOEBE WASN'T SURE why she'd taken the detour on her way into work on Friday, but she'd had the sudden need to swing by Vivien's Armoire. The lingerie store was just opening for the day, and the only person inside was the blonde who'd helped Phoebe before.

Wren was arranging a display of boyfriend shorts and glanced up with a welcoming smile that warmed into an even more genuine greeting. "Hey, I remember you! How was…" She paused, frowning. "I want to say Florida?"

"Miami. And it was great," Phoebe said hollowly. Possibly the most fun she'd ever had in her life. In contrast, the past day and a half had been a bleak absence of fun.

"Since you're back," Wren said knowingly, "I guess your friend liked the stuff you bought. We have some new items over there, and a sales rack by the fitting room."

"Thanks." As Phoebe meandered between the racks of lace and satin, she realized why she'd come. She wanted to recapture some of the free-spirited person she'd been in Miami, even though there was no man in her life. *I can buy pretty, provocative underwear just for my own enjoyment!* Who cared if she didn't have anyone to show it to? Yet despite the attempt at bolstering, she kept veering away from anything that reminded her of the pieces she'd packed for the trip. Instead, she found herself standing in the very back, looking at a wall of pajamas.

"All set?" Wren asked as Phoebe approached the cash register.

"Yep. I need to get to work myself, so this was just a quick trip."

"Well, come back any—" She blinked when she

saw what Phoebe set on the counter. "Damn, I didn't even know we carried flannel pajamas in June."

"They just look so soft. And comforting. Like a…" Her voice broke. "Like a hug."

Wren cocked her head to the side, her expression sympathetic. "So I guess Florida wasn't actually 'great?'"

"No, the trip really was great." Phoebe gave her a sad smile. "It's returning to reality that sucks."

13

KNOWING THAT IT was important for the kitchen staff to respect Cam, Heath made it a point not to disagree with the chef in front of everyone else. In the privacy of the managerial office, however, it was a different story. He loosened his tie, waiting for Cam to close the door behind him.

"That was not the menu we agreed to tonight," Heath said. There'd been more cost-effective ways to use the seafood, but Cam liked to concentrate on flavors rather than the budget. It was why they were partners. If Cam opened his own place, he'd be bankrupt inside a month.

"I don't remember us 'agreeing.'" Cam stood with his arms folded, glaring down at Heath behind the desk that ate up most of the space in the small room. "What I remember is you barking orders at me."

"I'm doing my job." In the past, Heath had always been able to lose himself in work. But his refuge seemed to be failing him at the moment. "You—"

"It isn't just me. You've been barking at everyone. Maybe you should rethink working front of house until your mood improves. The middle of the week is slow—take tomorrow night off and spend it with that brunette you're seeing."

"You want me out of the way so you can cook whatever you feel like, to hell with the consequences. And, not that it's your concern, but Jessa and I aren't seeing each other. We went on a couple of dates. They weren't leading anywhere."

Cam shot him a look of pure disgust. "So you got bored already, huh? Shocker."

"What is your problem? I took a nice lady out a few times, we had no chemistry and I won't be calling her again." That was all the information Cam needed about his love life. Heath didn't share how, when she'd ordered sorbet after their last dinner, he'd all but faked an illness to cut the evening short. Sorbet reminded him of Miami. Of Phoebe.

He couldn't think about her yet. *So what's the plan?* To give up desserts because they might remind him of his favorite pastry chef? To spend the rest of a hot Atlanta summer avoiding the pool because he wouldn't be able to dive into the water without hearing the splash of her bikini bottoms next to him? He associated her with baseball and balconies and planes. Hell, he couldn't look at the mirror hanging in his own living room without thinking about her. Maybe he should put it on Craigslist.

"Whoa." Cam rocked back on his heels, his eyes wide. "You really are miserable, aren't you? Is this…"

His expression turned wary and he took a step back toward the door before asking, "Is this about Phoebe?"

Her name sliced through him. He ground his teeth. "If you gloat about getting her back, I will find a way to kill you and make it look like a kitchen accident."

Cam laughed out loud and Heath was halfway to his feet when the chef held up his hands in a placating gesture. "Dude, we *aren't* back together."

A dozen emotions hit him at once. He didn't know if he was relieved or even more depressed. *So she didn't choose him. She just chose* not *to be with me?* "But I thought…"

"Yeah. I had that same misconception." Cam winced. "She set me straight pretty fast, though. Phoebe definitely doesn't want to date me. Odd that she doesn't want you, either. I thought no woman turned down the great Heath Jensen."

"Make your jokes, but you don't know what the hell you're talking about. This isn't the first time I've had my heart br—" He stopped dead, appalled at what he'd been about to say.

"Phoebe broke your heart?" Cam's jaw dropped. "Jesus, does that mean you actually love her?"

"I never said that." And he never would. Heath had no intention of making himself look like an ass. Or a stalker. He was all in favor of seducing a willing participant, but he refused to throw himself at an uninterested former lover.

Cam finally sank into one of the office chairs. "Now I'm confused. You are clearly crazy about her—"

"Get out. I'm sure we have some very expensive

ingredients in the pantry you can misuse. Go be fiscally irresponsible."

"But Phoebe seemed so sad on the drive home from the airport—which, as it turned out, had nothing to do with missing me. If neither of you are happy about splitting up, why did you?"

Heath shoved a hand through his hair. He'd been doing that a lot lately, and he knew without even looking in a mirror that it was standing on end and that he needed a shave. Add in the red-rimmed eyes he was developing from insomnia and he looked like a man who'd gone on a bender. *Maybe that's exactly what's happened.* Only, instead of booze, he'd been drunk on Phoebe—addicted to the way she felt and tasted. The sound of her laugh and her whoop of joy whenever her team scored. The twist of her smile whenever she was thinking something naughty.

Perhaps it was time to get literally drunk. Bourbon might temporarily dull some of those memories, and the majority of the staff had gone home. "Want to sit with me at the bar?" he invited Cam. Phoebe's ex wouldn't be his first choice of drinking buddies, but desperate times…

"No."

"Good. More for me."

"You are not going to sit around drinking up our booze. You are going home and figuring out a plan for getting Phoebe back."

"The hell I am." While most of his breakups had been amicable, there had been a few women who'd tried to hang on too long, who'd tried to convince him that they shared something that just wasn't there. He knew how horribly awkward it was, and he wasn't going through that with her.

Cam stood, shaking his head. "Listen to the voice of experience, man. If you throw away the chance to be with her, you'll regret it. I got complacent and gave her up because I was feeling a little bored with my life. I should have repainted my apartment or come up with some crazy new chef's tasting. She wasn't the problem, and losing her was one of the stupidest things I've ever done. You do not want to make the same mistake."

"There's a key difference. She's not mine to lose." And she never had been.

"Two weeks," Gwen said, pointing the remote control at the television. The screen went dark.

"Hey," Phoebe protested from her armchair, where she was snuggled under a comforter in her flannel pajamas. Wrapping herself in so many layers in the middle of summer required blasting the air-conditioner at arctic temperatures, but at least she felt cozy this way—shielded from her own love life and questionable decisions. "Our show was about to come back from commercial."

"We weren't really watching it. All I was doing was complaining about the makeup choices, and you were staring into space. Again. No doubt thinking about Heath, not that the bastard deserves a second thought from you."

Phoebe considered denying that her mind had been

on Heath, but what would be the point? Gwen knew her too well. "I didn't think about him for the first half of the show, but then the detectives went into that club to look for witnesses and it reminded me of this club we went to in Miami." Not that they'd been there for long. *Because I was too eager to get him back to the hotel room and all to myself.*

"With Cam, I gave you ten days to mope before I sent you back into the world of the living. And you were with Cam for years. How can it possibly take longer than that to recover from your ill-advised fling with his demon business partner?"

Maybe because it had been a hell of a lot more than a fling? She'd lost her heart to him, but if she admitted that to Gwen, her roommate would go ballistic and remind Phoebe that she'd known better. As it turned out, the advanced warning hadn't helped. She and Cam had been like a recipe, one that made sense on paper, and she'd followed all the measurements and instructions properly. The results had been good. She and Heath had been a creative flash, where she'd thrown caution to the wind, breaking the rules and adding spices that were almost counterintuitive but somehow complemented each other, and the results had been *magic.* Temporarily.

"Maybe we should handle this the way we did last time," Gwen said thoughtfully. "I sent you to Bobbi's looking glamorous and sexy to start the healing process with Cam. Maybe I should make us dinner reservations at Piri and—"

"Don't you dare!" Phoebe protested, surprised to

hear real anger in her voice. It was jarring to have an emotion penetrate the numbness. "Frankly, I'm surprised you haven't learned your lesson. My going to Bobbi's looking like that—and Heath kissing me—is what started all this." Gwen had made her a femme fatale for the night. Heath had bought in to the illusion and, driven by insecurity and heartbreak, Phoebe had asked him to help her make it a reality. But at the end of the day, she was still just Phoebe. That would have to be enough for the next man she fell for. *In ten or twenty years.*

Gwen sighed. "You're right. I never would have made you go to that party if I'd known Heath was finally going to make his move. Your defenses were down, and he went in for the kill."

"He went in for a *kiss*, drama queen. Wait—what do you mean 'finally' made his move?"

"I didn't trust the way he looked at you from the first night you introduced us," Gwen said. "Like he was just waiting for a chance to add you to his list of conquests."

"Are you saying," Phoebe asked slowly, "that he was attracted to me? *Before* Bobbi's?"

He'd told her that night how amazing, how different, she looked. She'd believed it was Gwen's makeover that had spurred his attraction. Was it possible he'd been drawn to her before, even when they'd worked together and she'd spent most of her time wearing a shapeless jacket and chocolate stains? *He never let me know.* But how could he, when she was with Cam? Given his past, she knew instinctively that Heath would never stoop to seducing another man's woman.

"Why would that matter now that he's dumped you?" Gwen demanded.

"You shouldn't paint him as the bad guy." She hadn't given Gwen specifics, just a general outline of events. "Our return to a platonic relationship was mutual."

"Oh, honey, it's never mutual. People say that to save face, but there's always one party who opens the escape hatch. Did he suggest it first, or did he get you to bring it up, make you think it was your idea?"

"But it *was* my idea." In order to keep him from hurting her, she'd launched a preemptive strike. At the time, it had felt like the right action to take. In retrospect, it felt more like…panic. "I told him that Miami had been fun, but it was probably best to just be friends once we got home." He hadn't tried to talk her out of it. Quite the opposite. He'd seemed pleased by the idea, reminding her of all the women who'd be happy to have him back in circulation.

Then again, he was used to playing the role of accommodating charmer. She'd watched him smile and soothe difficult customers, telling them what they wanted to hear, even when she knew he was angry on the inside.

"Oh, God, Gwen. What if, from Heath's perspective, I dumped him?"

Gwen hooted with laughter. "About time someone put his colossal ego in check!"

"Will you stop? He's a good man." She thought

about him chasing after that elderly woman at the ballgame with her purse, how he'd made a shy barista feel like the belle of the ball at that awards ceremony, the personal loan he'd given one of Piri's dishwashers six months ago when the man had wanted to get home to see his sick grandmother. Heath himself had rolled up his sleeves and helped with the dishes in the guy's absence. *And then there's everything he's done for me.*

She didn't want to become someone else in order to keep a man, but she *was* grateful that he'd shown her sides of herself she hadn't known existed.

Standing, she let the comforter fall and paced the living room, filled with nervous energy. Had she been wrong? Was there a chance for them? Maybe not, if she'd injured his pride. And it had been two weeks. Lord knew how many women he'd gone out with since that awful goodbye at the airport. The memory of him calling her "sweetheart" still turned her stomach.

"If you're finally shedding your ten-pound blanket, does that mean I can turn the A/C back to a civilized temperature? I went to use my mouthwash this morning and discovered it was freezing into mint-flavored slush."

"Gwen, I never thought I'd say this, but Cam was right to break up with me. I cared deeply about him, but it turns out he wasn't the one."

"Oh, hell." Gwen cradled her head in her hands. "I'm going to have to learn to like the demon, aren't I?"

"Yes, if I can figure out how to fix the mess I made."

Had Heath wanted a real relationship with her, or had it just been a fling? And even if his feelings had deepened, would he want to try again after she'd walked away?

Only one way to find out.

It was after midnight on Wednesday when Cam opened the kitchen's back door and let Phoebe inside. He looked ridiculously relieved to see her.

"Thank God you're here," he said, his voice low. "If his mood doesn't improve, I swear people are going to start quitting. He's in his office. I'll make sure no one disturbs the two of you and lock up on my way out."

"Thanks." She'd felt weird calling him after her epiphany with Gwen, but she'd wanted to find out if Heath was even at the restaurant. For all she'd known, he could have been on a date with the Kemp sisters. Cam had not only waved away any awkwardness, but he'd also been downright eager for her to get to Piri right away.

"No thanks necessary," he said. "You're doing me the favor. I can't open a second restaurant with the man if he self-destructs. The two of you getting back together may be the only way to save my career."

Despite the almost unbearable nerves churning through her, she chuckled at that. Cam could get a job tomorrow at half a dozen places. But she appreciated his support. His belief that Heath missed her had given her the courage to come over here tonight. *Before I can talk myself out of it.*

She nodded hello to a couple of her former coworkers who were headed home and took a deep breath as she padded down the short hallway. She glanced at the faded denim skirt that stopped just above her knees and hoped she hadn't made a tactical error. Gwen had taken one look at her and recoiled, demanding, "You're trying to win him back in a T-shirt and a ponytail? I mean, it's an improvement over the flannel PJs, but still... At least let me help you with some makeup!"

Phoebe had thanked her for the offer but firmly declined. She wouldn't be going to him as some upgraded version of herself or as a calculated seductress. Sure, it might have helped her cause if she'd appeared in his office wearing high heels and a trench coat with nothing underneath, but this felt a lot more honest. Over the past two weeks, she'd realized that in Miami she hadn't been honest enough with him—or herself.

The door was closed, and her own knock reverberated in the hall, making her jump.

"Come in," Heath called from the other side.

The moment of truth. She opened the door and tried to summon a smile. "Hi." At the moment, it felt like the most insipid word in the English language, but she had to start somewhere.

"Phoebe!" He got to his feet, looking stunned. But not necessarily happy. He recovered his composure quickly, though, giving her a neutral smile. "I hope you aren't here to ask about getting your old job back. James and I have a gentleman's agreement about me not stealing you away."

"Work is definitely not why I'm here," she said, closing the office door. This wasn't about going back; it was about moving forward. She hoped. "How are you?"

"Great, thanks."

That took some of the wind out of her sails. *What did you expect, dummy? That he was going to tell you he's been lost without you and counting the minutes since you've last seen each other?* That would have been nice. Trying to bolster her courage, she held onto Cam's assurances that Heath wasn't the same without her.

"And yourself?" he asked pleasantly. "How've you been?"

"I'm…" She chose her words carefully. The entire way over here, she'd tried to decide what to say to him, but this was harder than she'd expected, laying her heart bare while he stood there watching, his expression unreadable. "I'm regretful. I've been thinking a lot about what I said on the flight back from Miami, and I made a mistake."

Emotion flickered in his eyes and he came around the edge of the desk. At first she thought he wanted to be near her, and her heart leaped. But he went to the door and she realized he was going to try to send her on her way.

"Everything you said on the flight was completely sensible," he said. "You pointed out that we have a long-standing friendship and it was probably best for both of us if we returned to that."

"And friends ignore each other for two weeks?"

As painful as the thought was that he might not love her back, it was equally upsetting to realize that she may have lost his friendship, too.

"I'm sure we've both just been busy, me trying to get things off the ground for Hot and you putting in overtime to make up lost days for James. Maybe we can meet for lunch soon, but it's been a long day and—"

"Please don't," she said, laying her hand over his when he reached for the doorknob. "Heath, I screwed up, and I'm sorry. I was scared. Scared you wouldn't want me," she confessed in a whisper.

"Not want you?" He stalked away from her, angrily pacing. "Jesus, Phoebe, how many more ways could I possibly have shown you how much I wanted you? I couldn't keep my hands off you."

The memory of how greedy they'd been for each other was bittersweet. "I know, but how many relationships that start with that kind of passion can sustain it? And your track record with women— This is about me, though," she hastily amended, not wanting to sound as if she blamed him for her insecurities. "You know the story of Cinderella? I felt like that flight back from Miami was my midnight. I adored being sexy for you, but in my real life, I don't wear high heels. I don't skinny-dip. I don't have huge blocks of time free in my schedule to while away the hours having sex. And I was afraid that once I got back to being regular, everyday Phoebe…"

A muscle ticked in his jaw. "You must not have a very high opinion of my intellect. You don't think I know who 'regular' Phoebe is? You don't think I'm capable of seeing your beauty when you're in a chef's jacket and sneakers instead of a dress with a scandalous neckline?"

His calling her beautiful would have felt like more of a triumph without the wealth of accusation in his tone.

"Heath, please understand, I grew up feeling unwanted, with it hanging over my head every day. Cam dumping me just reinforced insecurities I didn't even realize ran so deep. And then there was you." She reached a hand toward him, but he rocked back on his heels, avoiding her touch, clearly still mad. Okay— anger she could work with. Anger was better than indifference.

"When you made love to me, you made me feel more wanted—more cherished and adored—than I have in my entire life. Which was terrifying because that meant I had to acknowledge how much it would hurt when you *stopped* wanting me."

"Who says I'm the one who would have stopped? *You* pushed *me* away." But his gaze softened and she knew he was at least considering her explanation.

"I know, and I'm sorry. But when I suggested that we return to platonic friendship, you didn't waste any time agreeing with me! You all but pulled out your phone and started texting all the women in your contact list that you were available again."

His gaze was stony. "I have my pride, Phoebe."

And she'd injured it. Maybe the best way to get through to him was to put her own pride on the line. She recalled his teasing explanation at the awards luncheon of how they'd started dating, words that had been meant as a joke. But despite the playful smile she gave him, the underlying sentiment was genuine.

"I want you desperately," she said, advancing toward him. "I need you, I crave you…and I love you."

"Phoebe." He didn't just meet her halfway—he lunged for her, pulling her into his arms. His mouth crushed hers in an ardent, uninhibited reunion that made her heart sing. She resented the two weeks she'd let pass before coming to him. Why had she waited?

Oh, yeah, because she'd been terrified he might not feel the same way. Technically, he still hadn't said as much, although she took his kiss as a good sign. She and Heath were fantastic together, and they both knew it. She refused to let fear cheat her out of that.

Placing her hands on his shoulders, she lightly shoved, urging him into the wide leather chair behind them. Then she straddled his lap, her skirt riding up as she bent forward to kiss him again.

He nipped at her lower lip with his teeth. "God, I've missed you." He was already growing hard beneath her, and she sighed at how good he felt. Desire simmered through her, even more potent than before because of the emotions magnifying it.

"I missed you, too." She brushed kisses along his neck, toward his ear. "Let's avoid that by sticking together from now on. I know you may still be upset that I pushed you away, but I have some ideas on earning your forgiveness." She rolled her hips, moving against him.

He groaned. "How could I say no? I've fallen in love with you, Phoebe Mars."

His declaration incited her more than any touch could, and she lifted herself off his lap just enough to fumble with the button at the front of his pants. He palmed her breast through her T-shirt while kissing the hollow of her throat, and the tremble that went through her didn't help her dexterity. Coming to her aid, he unzipped the pants while she stood to shimmy free of her underwear and get a condom from the purse that had hit the floor. She unrolled it over his rock-hard erection, gently squeezing the shaft and reveling in the way his eyes darkened with desire. The lean planes of his face were taut with tormented pleasure, his expression one of raw masculine beauty.

Anticipation thrummed through her, mingled with the emotions she felt for him, this man who saw and accepted her as she was while also helping her discover new facets of herself.

"I love you," she murmured, lowering herself onto his cock and taking him deep.

She tightened around him and they moved together, their pace as urgent as their need for each other. The chair beneath them creaked loudly in protest. The two of them were probably the only ones left in the building, but if not, Phoebe couldn't bring herself to be bothered by the idea that people knew she and Heath were making love. She felt gloriously unashamed.

Her climax began to spiral through her, and Heath muffled her involuntary shout with a kiss, then followed her over the edge. Her head fell forward, resting on his shoulder, and they sat there in almost dazed silence, their only sounds ragged breathing.

"Let's never move from this spot," she said, mellow and lethargic with satisfaction.

He chuckled. "That's going to make the meeting I have scheduled in the morning a little awkward." He caught her chin between his fingers, tilting her face to his for a kiss so tender that she found herself blinking teardrops off her lashes.

"You really forgive me for what I said on the plane?" she asked.

"I do, as long as you forgive me. I should have fought harder for us—like you did tonight." He grinned. "I don't know if I'm scared of the fights we'll have in the future because I already know you'll win, or if I'm eager because I look forward to how we'll work out those disagreements. Your powers of seductive persuasion are undeniable."

"Well—" she winked at him "—I learned from the best."

* * * * *

Be sure to look for Tanya Michaels's next Harlequin Blaze novel, available in 2017 wherever Harlequin books and ebooks are sold!

COMING NEXT MONTH FROM

Available June 21, 2016

#899 COWBOY AFTER DARK
Thunder Mountain Brotherhood
by Vicki Lewis Thompson
Liam Magee is at the ranch for a wedding—so is Hope Caldwell, whom he's wanted in his bed for months. Hope craves the sexy cowboy but can she trust him for more than a fling?

#900 MAKE MINE A MARINE
Uniformly Hot!
by Candace Havens
Having recently returned home, Marine Matt Ryan is looking forward to a more peaceful life as a helicopter instructor at the local base...not realizing free-spirited Chelly Richardson is about to rock his world!

#901 THE MIGHTY QUINNS: THOM
The Mighty Quinns
by Kate Hoffmann
Hockey player Thom Quinn has never hesitated to seduce a beautiful woman. But the bad boy has to be good this time, because Malin Pederson controls his fate on the team. And she's the boss's daughter.

#902 NO SURRENDER
by Sara Arden
Fiery Kentucky Lee burns hot enough to warm Special Ops Aviation pilot Sean Dryden's frozen heart—not to mention his bed—but he must NOT fall for his ex-fiancée's best friend...

YOU CAN FIND MORE INFORMATION ON UPCOMING HARLEQUIN® TITLES, FREE EXCERPTS AND MORE AT WWW.HARLEQUIN.COM.

HBCNM0616

REQUEST YOUR FREE BOOKS!
2 FREE NOVELS PLUS 2 FREE GIFTS!

HARLEQUIN®

Blaze

red-hot reads!

YES! Please send me 2 FREE Harlequin® Blaze® novels and my 2 FREE gifts (gifts are worth about $10). After receiving them, if I don't wish to receive any more books, I can return the shipping statement marked "cancel." If I don't cancel, I will receive 4 brand-new novels every month and be billed just $4.74 per book in the U.S. or $5.21 per book in Canada. That's a savings of at least 14% off the cover price. It's quite a bargain. Shipping and handling is just 50¢ per book in the U.S. and 75¢ per book in Canada.* I understand that accepting the 2 free books and gifts places me under no obligation to buy anything. I can always return a shipment and cancel at any time. Even if I never buy another book, the two free books and gifts are mine to keep forever.

150/350 HDN GH2D

Name	(PLEASE PRINT)

Address		Apt. #

City	State/Prov.	Zip/Postal Code

Signature (if under 18, a parent or guardian must sign)

Mail to the **Reader Service:**
IN U.S.A.: P.O. Box 1867, Buffalo, NY 14240-1867
IN CANADA: P.O. Box 609, Fort Erie, Ontario L2A 5X3

Want to try two free books from another line?
Call 1-800-873-8635 or visit www.ReaderService.com.

* Terms and prices subject to change without notice. Prices do not include applicable taxes. Sales tax applicable in N.Y. Canadian residents will be charged applicable taxes. Offer not valid in Quebec. This offer is limited to one order per household. Not valid for current subscribers to Harlequin Blaze books. All orders subject to credit approval. Credit or debit balances in a customer's account(s) may be offset by any other outstanding balance owed by or to the customer. Please allow 4 to 6 weeks for delivery. Offer available while quantities last.

> **Your Privacy**—The Reader Service is committed to protecting your privacy. Our Privacy Policy is available online at www.ReaderService.com or upon request from the Reader Service.
>
> We make a portion of our mailing list available to reputable third parties that offer products we believe may interest you. If you prefer that we not exchange your name with third parties, or if you wish to clarify or modify your communication preferences, please visit us at www.ReaderService.com/consumerchoice or write to us at Reader Service Preference Service, P.O. Box 9062, Buffalo, NY 14240-9062. Include your complete name and address.

HB15

SPECIAL EXCERPT FROM

HARLEQUIN
Blaze

*Liam Magee is at the ranch for a wedding—so is
Hope Caldwell, who he's wanted in his bed for months.
Hope craves the sexy cowboy, but can she trust him
for more than a fling?*

Read on for a sneak preview of
COWBOY AFTER DARK*, the second story of 2016 in
Vicki Lewis Thompson's sexy cowboy saga*
THUNDER MOUNTAIN BROTHERHOOD*.*

Hope was a puzzle, and he didn't have all the pieces
yet. Something didn't fit the picture she was presenting
to everyone, but he'd figure out the mystery eventually.
Right now they had a soft blanket waiting. He lifted her
down and led her over to it.

He'd ground-tied both Navarre and Isabeau, who were
old and extremely mellow. The horses weren't going
anywhere. Hope sat on the blanket like a person about
to have a picnic, except they hadn't brought anything to
eat or drink.

Liam decided to set the tone. After relaxing beside
her, he took off his Stetson and stretched out on his back.
"You can see the stars a lot better if you lie back."

To his surprise, she laughed. "Is that a maneuver?"

"A maneuver?"

"You know, a move."

"Oh. I guess it's a move, now that you mention it." He
sighed. "The truth is, I want to kiss you, and it'll be easier
if you're down here instead of up there."

"So it has nothing to do with looking at the stars."

"It has everything to do with looking at the stars! First you lie on your back and appreciate how beautiful they are, and then I get to kiss you underneath their brilliant light. It all goes together."

"You sound cranky."

"That's because nobody has ever made me break it down."

"I see." She flopped down onto the blanket. "Beautiful stars. Now kiss me."

"You just completely destroyed the mood."

"Are you sure?" She rolled to her side and reached over to run a finger down his tense jaw. "Last time I checked, we still had a canopy of stars arching over us."

"A canopy of stars." He turned to face her and propped his head on his hand. "Did you write that?"

"None of your beeswax."

Although she'd said it in a teasing way, he got the message. No more questions about her late great writing career. "Let's start over. How about if you lie back and look up at the stars?"

"I did that already, and you didn't pick up your cue."

"Try it again."

She sighed and rolled to her back. "Beautiful stars. Now kiss—"

His mouth covered hers before she could finish.

Reading Has Its Rewards

Earn **FREE BOOKS!**

Register at **Harlequin My Rewards** and submit your Harlequin purchases from wherever you shop to earn points for free books and other exclusive rewards.

Plus submit your purchases from now till May 30th for a chance to win a $500 Visa Card*.

Visit **HarlequinMyRewards.com** today

MYR16R1

Whatever You're Into... Passionate Reads

Looking for more passionate reads from Harlequin®?
Fear not! Harlequin® Presents, Harlequin® Desire and
Harlequin® Blaze offer you irresistible romance stories
featuring powerful heroes.

◆HARLEQUIN *Presents.*

Do you want alpha males, decadent glamour and jet-set
lifestyles? Step into the sensational, sophisticated world of
Harlequin® Presents, where sinfully tempting heroes ignite a
fierce and wickedly irresistible passion!

◆HARLEQUIN *Desire*

Harlequin® Desire novels are powerful, passionate and
provocative contemporary romances set against a backdrop of
wealth, privilege and sweeping family saga. Alpha heroes with
a soft side meet strong-willed but vulnerable heroines amid a
dramatic world of divided loyalties, high-stakes conflict and
intense emotion.

◆HARLEQUIN *Blaze*

Harlequin® Blaze stories sizzle with strong heroines and
irresistible heroes playing the game of modern love and lust.
They're fun, sexy and always steamy.

Be sure to check out our full selection of books
within each series every month!

www.Harlequin.com

HPASSION2016